AF485307

Holiday Mayhem: All I Wanna Be Is Tru

Kayla Isaac

Copyright © 2020 Kayla Isaac
Published by T'Ann Marie Presents, LLC
All rights reserved. No part of this book may be reproduced in any form without written consent of the publisher, except brief quotes used in reviews.
This is a work of fiction. Any references or similarities to actual events, real people, living or dead, or to real locals are intended to give the novel a sense of reality. Any similarity in other names, characters, places, and incidents are entirely coincidental

Chapter 1

BORN TIRED

Tru

"Siempre estoy tan feliz de tener a la familia aquí, estoy feliz de que finalmente los hayas comprado, Adrian!" my husband's mother exclaimed.

"Mamá inglesa, habla inglés." Adrian laughed lightly, taking a sip of his Merlot.

"I'm sorry, it's just it feels like it's been forever since I've seen you, Tru, and Royal."

"I know. How long has it been? Two years." I smiled, reaching over, placing my hand on top of hers.

"Si, yes. Two long years." She laughed, giving me a warm smile.

After flying almost three hours from Florida to Cancun, I was beyond ecstatic to be back on the ground, new grounds, to be specific. My husband Adrian and I haven't seen his parents in a while, and due to the holidays slowly approaching, we decided to take a trip to Cancun to visit them. Adrian's mother was the owner of her own restaurant here in Mexico, with a few others in surrounding areas, where his father owned a contracting company.

"I see my neita has grown up quite a few." She smiled, looking over at my daughter Royal who was punishing the plate of homemade swiss enchiladas in front of her.

"She has. She's a handful too. I might have to leave her down here sometimes." I laughed, looking at the sudden facial expression change on my daughter's face.

"That's not a bad idea. Maybe I can help her with her Spanish."

"Of course, I mean she has a Spanish tutor, but personally learning from her grandmother would be a wonderful experience."

"Great, we can discuss it in the future."

"You know what else we can discuss in the future? More grandkids," Adrian's father, Julius, chimed in.

"Oh Lord, dad, we have this conversation every time we talk."

"Well, you and Selena are our only kids. Your sister made it clear that she doesn't want kids because she's focusing on her soccer career. One more grandchild won't hurt."

"Speak for yourself. Childbirth is something serious." I laughed, shaking my head.

We conversed about everything under the moon and stars until it was time to call it a night. Once Royal was put to sleep, I sat outside on the balcony, looking over at the beautiful view. Since Adrian was sitting in his father's man cave with him, his mother and I were on the balcony sipping on mimosas enjoying the beautiful Cancun weather. The sly breeze from the ocean whipped past my skin like a feather.

"It's so beautiful out here," I voiced, taking a sip from my flute.

"I know, that's why Julius and I decided to retire here instead of moving away from home. How are things back in Jacksonville?"

"Things are great."

"I'm happy for you."

"Thank you, Mrs. Montoya." I smiled, leaning over in my chair, giving her a side hug.

"How many times do I have to tell you to call me mom? Sweetheart, you are mi familia. You are such a beautiful, intelligent woman, and I'm so happy my son found someone like you. You know he's changed a lot since you two got together."

"How so?"

"You saved him, mi hija. He was in such a dark place before you two met. I'm so happy he's finally happy, you know?" She smiled.

"I know. I remember you telling me."

"So what are you all doing for the holidays? I know you're going to be with your family, but are you going to be with them for Thanksgiving, Christmas, and New Year's Day?"

"Thanks to Adrian, I will be." I sighed, really settling the fact in my mind that I would be with my family for the holidays. I haven't been around any of them in years, and I had my reasons. My family was a group of hypocritical, judgmental, manipulative liars who were stuck in their old ways. They were always trying to outdo one another, and I saw it personally growing up 'til the day I stepped foot out of my parents' house.

"Why that look?" she pressed.

"It's just, I haven't spoken to my family in a while now, and it feels weird knowing that time is approaching, and I'll be heading to South Carolina soon."

"Do you and your family not get along?"

"You don't know the half of it?" I laughed lightly, mainly to myself, downing the rest of my mimosa.

"Talk to me, mi hija," she replied, placing her hand on top of mine, giving me her undivided attention.

"My family is a handful. I haven't seen my parents since Royal was born, and the last time I saw my siblings was at my little brother's high school graduation. My family can be something else. Sometimes I wish they were all like you guys. You all are so laid back and supportive, and that's something I've been craving my entire life. My family never gave me support or love, and growing up in a Southern Christian household, I had to learn things the hard way. I was raised in a household that consisted of proving yourself to people who couldn't care less about you. I made good grades, sang in the church choir, hosted bible study, watched my siblings day in and day out while my parents left to live their lives. I can say I never lived my life the way I wanted growing up, and it shows. It's just I've changed so much since last time seeing my family, and I'm just nervous."

"Dios mío, lo siento mucho (Oh my god, I'm so sorry)," she gasped, getting up from her seat and pulling me into a hug.

"It's okay, I'm fine. I think I'm doing pretty well for myself now."

"You are. You are a beautiful, smart girl, and I'm sorry you had to go through that. I know this is the last thing you wanna hear, but mi hija, familia is very important. I know you don't have a good relationship with them, but you have a daughter. Show Royal how it looks to be around family because in the end, you're going to need them, and eventually, they're going to need you. When you leave to be with your family, try your best and find reconciliation. Once you find reconciliation, you'll feel so much better. Trust me."

"Thank you."

"Anyway, sweetheart, I'm going to call it a night. Get some rest, you have a long trip ahead of you, and I'm not talking about traveling," she replied, kissing my forehead and walking off.

I sighed, staring off into space, thinking back to everything my family put me through. I went out of my way to show them how smart and determined I was every day, and they showed me each day how I wasn't important. Even after having a thriving career and being married to a man who has his stuff together, I still wasn't enough. When my career skyrocketed, I bought my parents a nice, big house, and both of them chose a car they wanted. I didn't even receive a simple "thank you" or "I'm proud of you" after doing that. I was never enough, and growing up, that really did a number on me. When I suffered from depression, I suffered on my own.

I suffered from anxiety as well, and I had to get through it all alone. My family didn't know what I went through, and it was sad. I even tried to kill myself on my sixteenth birthday because my parents didn't show me the attention and love I needed on a day that was really important to me. It seemed as if the more financially stable I grew, the more I grew essential to them. Not just my parents, but my grandmother, grandfather, aunts, uncles, and cousins. I was just a meal ticket to them, and now that I was no longer that, I was just "Little Bougie Ms. Stuck-up Tru who's better than everyone else".

They were never there, and it showed. I felt as if my siblings received the most attention, and even 'til this day, my parents adored them more than me. My siblings never had to go through what I went through, and none of them live with the same issues I have growing up in our household. All my siblings had a decent relationship with my parents except for me. My father and I were cordial, but my mother was the main issue. Sometimes I wish I were as fine internally as my siblings were then. They were all mentally and emotionally fine, but I was the damaged one. I was the hurt one, and it hurt just thinking that I had to force a smile for the holidays and pretend that everything was okay when it wasn't.

Chapter 2:

CRASHING PLANES

Syaire

So tell me, who's to blame?
Oh, who's to blame?
When we know that we've overstayed
Tell me who's to blame
~Lyrica Anderson

BEEP, BEEP, BEEP, BEEP!

I let out a groggy groan before reaching over to my dresser, pressing dismiss on my iPhone 11 before it could wake my husband. Looking over at him, I admired how peacefully he slept after the intense session of lovemaking we had last night. Getting out of bed, the sounds of my stiff bones cracking made me roll my eyes. I was a stay-at-home mother, and it showed. Even though a small selection of others may think it wasn't hard to juggle a job and raise kids, it took a toll on my body. With all three of my kids having extracurricular activities, alongside giving them all my undivided attention, it was a handful.

I walked into the bathroom, looking into my full body mirror. I looked down at my slim thick figure, something I found myself doing every morning. Going over to the window, I pulled back the sheer white curtains, letting the sun drape over my almond toned skin. Taking a deep breath, I opened the window, inhaling the fresh scent of the pine and taking in the sweet Tennessee breeze. It was something about taking in mother nature in the early mornings that gave me peace before my day started. Getting knocked from my trance, the sound of my phone going off made me tiptoe with caution back into my bedroom and grab it before it woke my husband.

Heading back into the bathroom, I answered the phone without looking at the caller ID.

"Hello?"

"Hi baby girl, just calling to check on you. You said you were going to call me back last night and never did," my mother, Tiffany, greeted.

"Oh, I'm sorry, mama. After putting the kids to sleep, I got tired and forgot."

"You're fine. All is forgiven. I was calling to tell you that I finally got Nora to answer her phone. She said she'll be here for the holidays."

"Hmm, that's odd. I thought the flashing lights and the famous life was more important than family to her. You know she always put the family on the back burner since she got famous."

"Don't do that. She's just busy."

"Just like Tru, I see. When was the last time you talked to her?"

"I didn't. Your father spoke to her. She's coming." She sighed.

"Why the sigh?"

"I just want the holidays to go great, you know. I don't want no drama or no issues. You know how hard it is to get our family together."

"I know, and it will go great mama, trust and believe that. We haven't seen Tru in years, so hopefully, things go well when we see her. You know how she acts? She always been stubborn and thought she was better than everybody else."

"You can say that again," my mother scoffed.

"Is she still with that Mexican boy?" I asked, leaning on the counter.

"She is."

"Something's off about that boy. You know, when I have a gut feeling, I always follow it. I don't trust him as far as I could throw him. I even told her to leave him, but she claims I'm jealous of her and that I wanna ruin her happiness. Baby girl, I have nothing to be jealous about. I've been married for eight years to the love of my life and have three beautiful babies. I have a successful career and a big house. I'm not jealous of you."

"She has a good career and a big house too, Syaire. I'm not trying to down talk her, but sometimes Tru feels as if she has to be entitled to everything. The last time we talked, she rubbed the house that she bought your father and me in my face. As I said, I don't talk with her like that unless I have to."

"I understand completely. When we got into it about Adrian, she tried me. She came for my husband and me."

"She brought up his age?"

"You know that's what she did, and I want everybody to keep the age jokes to themselves this year. Todd says it doesn't bother him, but it bothers me. He's a good man, and he takes care of his kids and me. I don't need him feeling uncomfortable every time we get around family."

"Todd's a good man, but I agree with everyone else, Syaire. I told you from the first day you brought him to meet the family, that man is too old for you."

"Mama, he loves me, and I love him. Age is just a number, and he's a good man."

"Syaire, your twenty-eight, and Todd is fifty-three. Let's not even get started on the fact that this man is white. I thought you would have married a black man."

"Okay, and?"

"Okay, I'll leave it alone," she replied in defeat.

"Look, I gotta go. I'll see you soon, mama."

"See you soon, sweetheart. I love you and don't be stressin'."

"Stressing? Me, I'd never."

"I'm serious, Syaire."

"I know, okay, mama, I gotta go. I love you."

Hanging up the phone, I looked up in the doorway to see Todd leaning on the doorframe in his Calvin Klein boxers. I took in his beauty, just thinking about how blessed I was to be with someone as generous, kind, and handsome as him. He may have been up in age, but he didn't look like it. Todd stood at six foot two, towering over my five-foot-four frame. His arms and chest were covered in ink, and he kept his full head of hair dyed platinum blonde. He even stayed in the gym, and his body was something serious. He was the reason I lost as much weight as I lost.

When Todd and I first met, I weighed two hundred and sixty pounds. Todd started off as my gym partner because we worked together in the hospital, which led to something more. I went from weighing Jennifer Hudson's *Dreamgirls* weight to Sheila who met Troy in the Mountains weight. I was beyond happy with my progress, and so was he. We had drinks one night celebrating my weight loss journey, and things went up just like that. Todd was a great husband, a great father, and the most successful brain surgeon out. I had hit the jackpot, and it felt good.

"Good morning, love, how did you sleep?" he asked, approaching me, pulling me into his arms.

"I slept amazing. How did you sleep, honey?"

"I slept great, thanks to you." He smiled, pecking my lips.

"That's great, baby. We need to talk."

"About what?" he asked, going over to the sink, preparing to brush his teeth.

"So, as you know, we're going to South Carolina to spend the holidays with my family this year."

"Yes, love, I know."

"So I was thinking we surprise them?"

"With what? We don't have to surprise them all the time."

"Yes, we do, Todd. Okay, so hear me out."

"Oh god." He sighed, putting his electric toothbrush down, and leaning on the counter with crossed arms.

"So, for Christmas, I was thinking we surprise everyone with a one-week trip to Dubai."

"Dubai?"

"Yes, baby Dubai."

"You've already been there."

"But they haven't. Them country motherfuckers have never been anywhere classy. My parents have never been outside of South Carolina, and my ratchet ass cousins would love it. Plus, this would top all the other gifts I gave them. Come on, baby. Look, I can see it now. We can stay at the Bulgari Hotel & Resorts —"

"Syaire, sweetheart, that hotel is almost eight hundred dollars a night," he interrupted with wide eyes.

"Okay, and so? We got the money to do it. Tru bought my parents a damn house a few years ago, and I feel as if I could do more for them than that. I was thinking after the Dubai trip, we can take my parent's house shopping for a place outside of the trenches. I wanna do so much—"

"Syaire, love, we can't do that. Dubai? House searching outside of South Carolina. You just bought both of your parents a new Benz last year and five thousand dollars' worth of clothes. You even started your mother a Birkin bag collection like yours, and none of that is cheap. I'm sorry, but I'm not paying for a trip to Dubai for almost thirty of your family members. This isn't the first time we've had this conversation."

"So what your saying is, you want me to show up to my family embarrassed as if I don't have money like that. Like I'm some poor bitch?"

"Stop it, you know I didn't mean it like that," he replied, trying to touch my hand, but I pulled away.

"No, you stop it! I'll be damned if I sit here and let my other siblings sit here and try to out-do me. I'm not a poor stupid bitch that can't afford to treat her family. I worked my ass off day in and day out to try to prove myself to my family. You must not remember when I used to cry to you every night about them pressuring me to be the person that they want me to be. I'm Syaire mother-fucking Nelson. Syaire Garrett was struggling and was lost. But baby, I know where I am, and I know I'm nothing like the girl I used to be. Now, if I say I want tickets to Dubai for my family, I will get it. My family is gonna see that I'm above them now, and I always was. I'm never going to be second best again. I tell you that. The old Syaire they think is gonna show up for the holidays is down the drain, baby. I'm rich, bad, and bougie, and I don't have to question the price of something if I want it."

"You got one thing right, you aren't the Syaire that I used to know. I said I'm not paying for it." He sighed, with hurt all over his face.

Todd placed his toothbrush down, not even bothering to brush his teeth again. He shook his head at me before walking out of the bathroom, and I'm assuming to the bathroom downstairs. Letting out an angry groan, I stomped over to the door, slamming it shut and locking it.

This wasn't the first disagreement we've had with one another when it came to money. Since I was the oldest girl out of my parents' children, I was left with all the responsibility. However, when I got to a certain age, my mother sent me to Alabama with my great grandmother to grow up fast. One thing about me was since birth, I wasn't a pushover. If I didn't like something, I was gonna check you about it. No matter how many ass whipping I got when I was younger or punishments I got, I still had a hard head. My parents couldn't deal with it anymore, so they sent me to Alabama, where my great grandmother did exactly what they couldn't. She struck fear in me, and I listened to her as if I were a robot controlled by a remote. Since she was old school, she taught me about roots and witchcraft, and whenever I got out of hand, she always told me she would put a spell on me, and that shit scared me even 'til this day with her being six feet under.

She and I had a great relationship, and she taught me things I didn't know I needed to know. In her relationship with my grandfather, she always told me she was submissive to him and did what he wanted because she was taught by her mother and grandmother. Looking at that growing up, I wasn't having that shit. My great grandmother stayed in the same area since she was a little girl, and she lived life like a nun, but me, I wanted to get out and be out there. I wasn't about to be submissive to a man regardless of his status. I wasn't about to stay in one area 'til the day I die when there's an entire world out there to explore.

My parents may have encouraged me to do better in life, but they encouraged me to be the person they wanted me to be, not the person I wanted to be. When I saw how they were all over Tru, who followed everything they said, I'm not even gonna lie and say I wasn't jealous. When I noticed the attention Tru got, I started following in the footsteps my parents wanted me to follow in. Yeah, I may have had the career, the kids, the life, the money, and the perfect marriage. Still, I lacked the happiness, and I masked it every day. I found ways to cope, and even though it was unhealthy, I still needed that fix to get my right.

Running my hands down my face, I climbed on top of my counter, standing on my toes, opening the vent. I pulled out a bottle of Jack Daniels, taking it to the head. I knew I wasn't supposed to be drinking, and liquor wasn't even supposed to be in the house. Todd was a recovering alcoholic. He turned to alcohol once his wife and son died a long time ago, and I helped him get better. Now I was slowly easing in his footsteps, slowly turning into an alcoholic, and he didn't know. I felt like I was on a plane. Everything was going fine until I look up at the front to see the pilots are gone, and I'm slowly crashing into a mountain.

I've dealt with so much, and all I wanted to do was prove myself to my family, even if it meant flashing money that I knew they didn't have. They disapproved of so many things in my life, including my marriage with Todd, and here I am still trying to prove to them that I'm the daughter that made it out of the ghetto and doing better for herself. The thing was, I wasn't just drinking because my parents disapprove of things in my life, but I was also holding a secret so big it was killing me every day. And every year I spend time with my family for the holidays, the little girl in me just wants to yell it out. However, the adult in me is trying to kill it and continue life. I guess that's how it felt to be on a crashing plane, wanting to badly to get out, but you can't.

Chapter 3:

SUPERSTAR

Staying in the spotlight
Staying up past midnight
You stay on my mind
I'm trying to grind, alright
Married to the money
Fashion, Lights, and Fame
Never let nobody change the vision made
~IV Jay

"Yes! Give me face, Noni!" the photographer instructed.

"It's Nora, not Noni," I corrected him.

"I like Noni better."

"Don't feel some type of way. He thinks my name is Brandy, and it's Brittany," one of the models who was taking the photos with me chimed in.

After my photoshoot, I went to my vanity and stared back at the woman staring in the mirror. The last place I thought I would have been was here, modeling for an ankle bracelet line. A line that wasn't even poppin' at that. I remember back when I was the hottest new runway model out there. Now here I was, gathering up little gigs and trying to make a living. Part of me missed being in the spotlight, but one thing I didn't miss was the bad that came with it.

I remember the time I first went viral. I was on a semester break from college, and my girls and I decided to go out of town to a Nicki Minaj concert. After the show, we were invited to an after-party by the one and only Zay Money. Zay Money was a new artist in the music business that had everything jumpin'. When I bumped into him at the party, and we kicked it off, paparazzi snagged some photos of us on our first date. I was known as his mystery woman until we made it official. I was initially in college to become a teacher because I loved children, but that went straight out the window when Zay thought it would be perfect for me to model. He hooked me up to a few connections, and the next thing I knew, I was starting off on modeling Fashion Nova fits to being on magazine pages modeling for Rihanna's Fenty line.

When I got with Zay, I knew he was a player, and I thought I could have handled it. But apparently, the only person I was fooling was myself. When he cheated on me with one of my dearest friends, I broke things off with him. Even not being in a relationship, he carried my career and made sure I was making this model thing work. However, when he got sent to jail for drug trafficking, even with a promising career and money flowing in good, he still was stuck in his unintelligent hood ways. With him not being able to help me anymore, I was on my own. I lost Benz, my big house in the hills, and a few friends I made in the industry.

"Hey, you okay?" my friend Jessica quizzed, coming up behind me.

"Yeah, I'm straight." I sighed.

"It doesn't look like it."

"I'm fine."

"Okay, if you say so. You ready to dip?"

"Yeah, give me a minute."

Quickly putting on my shoes, I met Jessica outside and jumped in the passenger seat of her 2013 Hyundai Sonata. Instead of taking me straight home, we decided on getting lunch at Vito's Pizza.

"So, did you finally talk to your mom?" she asked.

"I did."

"And?"

"And nothing."

"Bitch, if you don't spill it."

"I'm going home for the holidays, Jess."

"Good, but did you tell your mom you're struggling?"

"She doesn't need to know that?"

"Oh wow, so she doesn't need to know that her baby girl is out in LA struggling like the crackhead in *New Jack City*. You need to tell her that your ass lost damn near everything. Don't sit here and act like you have shit together when you don't, and Samson ain't making shit no better. Is he still putting his hands on you?" she probed with frustration laced in her voice. She took a sip of her water, shaking her head at me.

"Don't worry about Samson and me, and don't worry about me in general. I'm a big girl, Jess."

"A big girl who gets her ass beat day in and day out by a nigga who ain't shit. I still think you a dirty bitch for fucking with him, knowing that he and Zay are tight. How does Zay feel about his homeboy beating on you?"

"That's enough."

"No, apparently it's not enough if you're still here. You know I only tell you this because I care about you. There's nothing wrong with being down, but there's something wrong with being down and being scared to ask for help. You have to get tired of this, Nora. He beats your ass, and then the little bit of gig money you make, he uses it to buy weed and smoke out y'all already roach-infested apartment. That nigga doesn't even pay bills. You need to ask your parents for help. There's nothing wrong with moving back home just until you get back on your feet. Don't you still wanna be a teacher? Go back to school."

"Look, if I wanted to be lectured, I would have asked you to do that. I don't ne—"

I was cut short by my cell phone ringing on the table. Samson's face flashed on the screen, making Jessie huff in annoyance.

"The devil's calling," she announced.

Ignoring her, I declined his call and placed my phone in my purse.

"Mind your business. I gotta go," I replied, getting up, leaving my money on the table to pay for my food.

"I could take you home, or you can just stay the night with me."

"I can Uber, thanks."

I grabbed my to-go cup and walked out of the restaurant, calling an Uber. Once it got there, the entire ride, I sat there thinking about why I didn't just decide to stay at Jess's place tonight.

When I got home, I saw a few cars in the parking lot that I knew too well. Swallowing the lump in my throat, I went inside my apartment. As soon as I opened the door, I heard Samson's deep baritone voice bounce off the walls. When he saw me, he smiled, showing his bottom grill. Samson stood six foot even compared to my five-foot-two frame. He was a dark skin treasure weighing two hundred thirty pounds of pure muscle. His chest was bare as a baby's bottom, and he always sports a fade. He was definitely something pleasurable to the eyes.

"I called," he said with low hooded eyes. I could tell he and his friends smoked a pound of weed before I got here. It wasn't only evident from how he looked, but he had my entire apartment lit up like the Fourth of July.

"I was working."

"What I tell you about lying to me?" he quizzed, walking over to me, backing me into the counter.

"I was busy. I'm sorry."

"You know how you can show me your sorry."

"How?"

"We need the money for rent this week. That bitch ass landlord was up here early today. My boys got some mon—"

"No, you promised me. You said I didn't have to do that anymore," I interrupted, feeling my heart drop, already knowing what he was implying.

"I know what I said then, but this is what I'm saying now. The boys in the room waiting on you. Don't keep them waiting."

"Sam, I can—"

I was cut short by him grabbing me by my throat, pushing my head to the wall.

"If I tell you to do something, you do it! You hear me!" he screamed in my face.

"Yes."

"Now get your ass in that room and make that money."

I felt as if I were about to walk *The Green Mile* on my way to the room. Before I could fully walk off, he grabbed me.

"Extra condoms are in the drawer. Do your thing, Superstar," he said, pecking my lips and letting me go.

Part of me just wanted to see how far I could run, but I knew I wouldn't make it. When I got to the room, three of Samson's best friends sat there, passing around a blunt.

"Well, well, well, if it ain't Ms. Superstar herself. We've been waiting for you."

All three men surrounded me before one of them reached in his pocket and pulled out a black Ziploc bag.

"You know the drill," he said, before putting a bit of the white substance that was in the bag on his pinky finger and putting it up to my nose.

Taking a hit and loosening up, I didn't even feel as if I was there anymore. My body was there, and they were doing whatever they wanted to me, but my soul and mind left as soon as my back hit the bed. The time couldn't get here fast enough for me to head home. I couldn't show them the lost strung-out Nora, who sold herself out. I had to show them top tier model Nora, the superstar.

Chapter 4:

PERFECT

Two Days Before Thanksgiving

"Baby, can you please stop shaking your leg? You're making me nervous." Adrian laughed, placing his hand on my shaking leg.

We had just reached South Carolina, and we were getting closer and closer to my hometown, Charleston. The closer we got to Moncks Corner, the more nervous I grew. It felt comforting coming in at first, looking at all the country life and reminiscing on growing up here.

"I'm sorry, it's just I'm nervous."

"Well, stop it. They're just your family. Baby, I'm here if you need me, and you know that. It can't be as bad as you think it is. Just calm down, breath in and breath in," he encouraged, looking over at me with that perfect smile of his that always seemed to lighten up my day. Doing just like he said, I calmed down, running my hands through my hair.

"I'm calm."

"I hope so." He laughed.

"I am, I promise."

"So how do you think Thanksgiving is gonna go with your family getting together?"

"Hopefully, it goes well."

"It will."

"Babe, can I ask you something?"

"Yeah, wassup?"

"Promise me something?"

"Anything?"

"If things get out of hand, don't argue with me. Just grab your stuff, and we head back home."

"Is that what you really wanna do? It's like you want something to pop off for us to go back home."

"I don't."

"Okay, then."

"Still, I want you to promise me."

"Fine, I promise." He sighed.

"Don't do that."

"Do what?"

"Act aggravated with me."

"I'm not aggravated with you."

"You acting like it."

"Shut up."

"No, you shut up."

"Quit playing with me, Tru." He laughed jokingly.

"And if I don't."

"You know I can't say what I wanna say with Royal in this car."

We shared a laugh before stopping to get gas. Since my parents' house wasn't far from the gas station, it only took us three minutes to get there, literally. When we pulled into the yard, my mother and Syaire were laughing it up, eating finger sandwiches and drinking pink lemonade, while Syaire's kids ran around the yard chasing my parents' Miniature Schnauzer and Shih Tzu. It seemed as if I was the elephant in the room because all eyes were on me as soon as I stepped foot out of the car.

My mother's face turned from happy and cheerful to subtle yet shocked. It felt as if everything on the inside wanted to move, but I couldn't find it in me to put one foot out that door. After Adrian woke Royal up and got her out of the car, he came to my side and opened the door. Helping me out of the car, he held my hand as we walked up to my mother and sister.

When I got closer to her, I took in her beauty. Beauty could be something crazy. It could look like heaven on the outside and be pure hell on the inside. My mother still looked exactly the same, and I was praying her attitude and old ways weren't. She blatantly stared at me, just taking in the fact that I was actually here.

"Tru." She smiled, pulling me into a hug.

I embraced her back, inhaling the scent of her Marc Jacobs perfume. She pulled away before caressing my cheek and putting one of my fallen loose curls behind my ear.

"I'm happy you're here," she voiced.

"It feels good to be here." I lied.

I wasn't about to sit here and act as if her greeting to me wasn't off. She usually had a snarky remark waiting for me. However, this woman I was standing in front of gave me a completely different vibe. Our moment was interrupted by Syaire clearing her throat.

"Tru," she said, greeting me with a head nod.

"Syaire," I replied, giving her the same energy.

"How was Cancun with Adrian's family?" my mother asked, linking her arms with mine, leading me away from Adrian and Royal for privacy.

"It was fine, mama."

"You sure?"

"Yes, why wouldn't it be?" I replied with a raised eyebrow.

"I'm still uneasy with you being around them when I haven't even met them."

"See, and that's the reason why you haven't."

"What reason is that?"

"Mama, you're judgmental. Adrian's parents are as sweet as pie, and you would find any reason in the world not to like them people. They're like family to me."

"But they aren't your family. We are. I still don't like how you're around his family all the time, and we have to drag you here against your will for you to finally decide to be with us."

"You don't have to drag me nowhere, mama, I'm a grown woman. I came because my husband insisted. I thought that little hug and the way you greeted me earlier was a hint you weren't going to be with your issues, but apparently, that was all a front."

"A front? Look, I don't know who you've been hanging around lately. I don't know if it's those saddity folks up there in Florida or them crazy behind Mexicans up there in Cancun, but I'm your mother, and you will not talk to me as if I'm one of those people off the streets, am I understood."

"Is everything okay?" Adrian asked, coming over in just the nick of time. I poked the inside of my cheek, not wanting to start any trouble my first day here.

"Understood," I replied to my mother before walking off into the house with Adrian on my trail. He pulled me by my arm, stopping me in my tracks.

"What was all that about? I thought everything was going good?"

"It was until she started her shit. Adrian, I don't think I'm gonna be able to keep my composure here for Thanksgiving, Christmas, and New Year's Day."

"Remember what I told you a while back?"

"No, I don't."

"Of course you don't remember because you were never going to do it. Baby, you gotta stick up for yourself and tell them how you feel."

"I can't."

"You can, baby, you got this."

"I hope I do."

"You do. Look, I'm about to go take Royal upstairs. Apparently, she's still tired from the ten-hour ride here."

"Okay, I'm gonna see where my daddy is."

"I think I heard your sister say he was in the backyard cooking on the grill."

"Okay, thanks, babe."

I pecked his lips before making my way through the house. Before I could get to the backyard, I heard a voice that I haven't heard in a long time.

"Oh shit, it must be a ghost. Is that my big sister Tru!" my little brother Marley yelled.

"You better stop all that cussin' in this house before mama kicks your behind." I laughed, bringing him into a hug.

"She does that every day."

"You really need to stop growing. Dang Marley, you're taller than me, and you're only sixteen."

"It comes in handy for basketball, big sis."

"How's that going?"

"It's going good. I really wish you would have been at my last game. Man, look, I took the team to the championship. You know I carry Berkeley County on my back when I get on that court." He smiled, showing his pearly whites.

"I know. I promise I'll be at the next one."

"Don't make a promise you can't keep."

"No, I'm serious. I used to always go to your games. Shoot, if it weren't for me, you wouldn't have even taken up basketball."

"I guess, and you're right about that. Basketball was the last thing on my mind."

"Exactly. You still hoeing around?"

"Hoeing around. Dang big sis, that's how you see me? I'm a well respectful, loyal gentleman. I don't be hoeing."

"Who do you think you're talking to? I be seeing you on Snapchat and Instagram with a different girl every week."

"Because I be jumpin'. You know how it is? You must not know the word around Berkeley High. The bitches love Marley." He smiled, popping his imaginary collar.

"Boy! If you don't watch your mouth in my house," my father warned, coming up behind Marley, popping him in the back of the head, making him flinch.

"My bad, pops."

"Yo bad my behind, go out there and help your uncles with that projector outside."

"Yes, sir," Marley replied, running off to do what he was told.

"I don't know what I'm gonna do with that boy right there," my father said.

"What can you do with him?" I laughed.

"How have you been, princess?"

"I've been well."

"That's good. I'm happy you're here." he replied, pulling me into his arms, embracing me so hard as if I would disappear if he let me go.

"I'm happy I'm here too. I missed you."

"I missed you too, honey. You're here just in time. Thanksgiving is in two days, and I know your aunties and mama is gonna have this kitchen smelling like a soul food restaurant. You can steal me some food."

"I can try. You know how they be over that pot."

"I know, but you're gonna be in the war zone to bring me a plate."

"I'm not getting in trouble for you, daddy." I laughed.

"What? All them times that I got in trouble for you."

"You did that on your own."

"Okay, and you can do that on your own as well. Come on, sneak your old man a piece of sweet potato pie or something. Shoot, some peach cobbler, some greens, some cornbread."

"Daddy, I'll try." I laughed, seeing how serious he was. I knew he was serious because one holiday he didn't play about was Thanksgiving.

"We need to catch up."

"Oh, do we?"

"Yes, we do. I need to know how that Adrian fella is treating my princess."

"He's treating me just like the queen I am."

"Good. Hey, I'm going to Walmart to pick up some stuff for Thanksgiving before these people raid the stores like the police. You wanna come?"

"As long as we take your Mustang."

"You know that's my baby. Come on, you driving?"

"Of course."

I followed my father out to the garage, waving at a few family members that I haven't seen in ages. He tossed me the keys to his baby blue 1966 mustang convertible. My dad was a sucker for older model cars. Even with a yard full of up-to-date vehicles that Syaire bought him and my mother, he drove his Mustang like it was the only car he had.

"Don't you dint my baby," he warned as we got in the car.

"I won't." I laughed, putting the key in the ignition.

"Daddy, where y'all going?" Syaire asked, coming into the garage with her arms crossed."

"To Walmart to go pick up some stuff."

"You didn't ask me if I wanted to come to Walmart with you. If you had to go to Walmart, you could have asked me when I first showed up."

"No, baby girl, it's fine. I also wanted to get some alone time with Tru."

"You didn't ask me if I wanted to get some alone time with you, daddy." Syaire pouted like a big kid.

"I can stay here, and you can go if you want," I suggested, trying to lighten her mood.

"I didn't ask you, Tru. I'm talking to daddy."

"Hey, stop that. I thought you wanted to spend time with your mama, Syaire?"

"I already did. I just felt as if we haven't spent time together since I got here yesterday."

"I promise we'll spend time soon. You're here for two months, sweetheart. We have plenty of time."

"If you say so."

"I'll see you later, sweetheart," my dad replied. Syaire stepped back and watched us pull out of the garage.

Chapter 5:

BEST PART OF ME

"Why you over here looking like a sad puppy?" my Aunt Carrissa asked.

"No reason."

"Niece, I know you. Try again. Now, what's wrong?" she quizzed once more, placing her hand on my shoulder.

"I said nothing. I'm fine. Don't you got somebody's palms to go read?" I scoffed, walking off.

"Yeah, your dirty ass palms, you rude heffa," she said loud enough for me to hear.

My Aunt Carrissa was my mother's little sister. She was the woke auntie who was into spiritual shit. She always kept a blunt between her lips. She claimed she was smoking herbs she grew, but we knew she smoked that Reggie off the corner. My Aunt Carrissa always wore boho-chic clothing and kept braids in her hair. Her ass got so high one time that she thought she was on another planet, and all of a sudden, her ass was into chakras and the spiritual shit. We never said anything about it because she always won the debate. It wasn't even my intention to be rude or distasteful toward her, but she, out of all people, knew if I was already aggravated, then don't converse with me if it was evident.

"Mommy, I'm tired," my daughter, Star, pouted.

"Okay, sweetie, go lay down."

"But I'm hungry too," she replied, pouting harder.

"Okay, baby, but didn't you just eat a sandwich earlier?"

"I didn't want that."

"Okay, then what do you want to eat, Star?"

"Oh no, you don't. Your bougie ass daughter needs to go right back to Tennessee," my Uncle Lewis said.

I'm surprised he didn't have that red plastic cup in his hand. This man would drink the ocean if it were made out of liquor if you let him. The way he and Star were mean mugging one another was priceless.

"Don't talk to my baby like that. What did she do?"

"She came to me telling me she was hungry, and I offered to buy her bougie ass some McDonalds, and she got the nerve to tell me she doesn't eat McDonalds. She told me she wants bruschetta. What the fuck is bruschetta? Then I tried to fix her ass some water out the tap, and her lil ass told me she doesn't drink water out the spigot. Then I tried to give her that Great Value bottle water, and she gonna mother fucking tell me she only drink Fiji water. I outta beat her ass."

"And I'm gone tell my daddy!" Star yelled, sticking her tongue out.

"And I'll beat your daddy's old ass. He's damned near the same age as me. Tell that white fucka to come at me."

"Uncle Lewis," I warned, pushing Star away from the conversation.

"But mama..."

"Go to the room and take a nap now," I scolded her.

Star pouted before stomping off toward the house. I crossed my arms, bringing my attention back to my uncle.

"What did I tell you about that?" I said, annoyed with how he talked to my daughter.

"Your daughter a lil bougie brat, and so is your son. That lil nigga told me he wants a Gucci jacket for Christmas. Boy, I don't even fucking own Gucci. I'll buy him some Coogi. You remember Coogi? They got the same color in the logo, so he won't know the difference."

"Uncle Lewis, please leave my kids alone."

"Your kids be fucking with me. The only one I like is Sunny. See, she can barely talk because she's only two. That Star and Tyreke is gonna make me break my prosthetic foot off in they asses."

"They are just kids."

"Bad ass kids," he scoffed.

"Mhm and stop threatening to fight my husband. Tod used to be an MFA fighter back in the day. Don't play my husband. Now he will break that prosthetic leg off and beat you with it."

"I wish his white ass would. Tell him to do it," he scoffed.

"Okay, baby, come here really fast," I replied, calling my husband over.

"Stop, what you doin'?"

"Calling him over."

"Yes, love?" Todd asked, jogging over.

"My Uncle Lewis got something to say to you." I smiled, watching my uncle look up at Todd. His ass was sweating bullets.

"Yes, I was just telling my niece that you're a very nice man, and I'm so happy that she found someone like you. Todd, you are such a respectful man, and I'm glad you're a part of our family."

"Oh, why, thank you, sir. I'm happy to be a part of your family. I tell Syaire every time that we should come visit more often."

"That would be nice. You and your kids are such a joy to be around."

"Thank you, well I'm gonna go help Mrs. Tiffany get some stuff out of the garage. It was nice talking to you."

"You too," my uncle replied, laughing awkwardly as Todd walked away.

"You sure told him." I laughed.

"Go to hell, Syaire."

"I love you too." I laughed.

"Mhm, so what was all that about with your sister and your daddy?"

"What are you talking about?" I replied, playing dumb.

"Don't play stupid with me child, I saw how you talked to Tru."

"Okay, and?" I replied, rolling my eyes.

"You were wrong for that. Tru was only trying to make your cry baby ass feel better. I watched you and your siblings grow up. You always treated that girl like a stepsister. Do me a favor. Don't run her away. We barely get to see her. You should have seen everyone's face when she walked in this yard."

"Wow, so I'm supposed to shut up and pretend to make Tru happy?"

"I never said that. Just act like she's your sister and not competition for once. I'm just happy that she's finally home."

"I don't get that reaction when I come home. No one's excited to see me."

"Shut your ass up. You come home damn near every two to three months. Your ass is not gone long enough for us to miss you. Stop acting like a goddamn child for once and be a big sister."

"I'm done with this conversation," I scoffed, walking away.

"Your ass is always done. Grow up, Syaire."

"Go to rehab, you drunk," I replied, flicking him off.

"The superstar is here!" Nora yelled, getting out of a limo with another woman getting out behind her.

Some of my family members looked in awe, while some looked with envy plastered on their faces. While walking over to her, I smiled, looking at the Gucci dress and matching pumps she had on.

"If it ain't the superstar." I smiled, walking over to her with open arms.

"In the flesh, baby."

"I haven't seen anything from you in a while. I haven't seen you in any new music videos or magazines lately."

"Girl, I'm on vacation. I needed a vacation from the fame. You should have seen the paparazzi when I left."

"I guess you found time to come and be around the family, I see."

"Girl, yes. I was so busy with photoshoots and award shows."

"Yeah, right," sneered the woman she came with.

"So who is this?" I asked.

"Oh, how rude of me. This is my best friend and assistant Jessica, but I call her Jess. Jess, This is my big sister Syaire."

"Nice to meet you, Syaire," Jessica said, extending her hand.

"Nice to meet you too, Jessica. Where you from?"

"I'm originally from Inglewood."

"Oh wow, welcome to South Carolina, sweetheart."

"Thanks, it's a lot different from Compton."

"I know. I've been to Inglewood a few times."

"You have?"

"Yup. I took my best friend there to take some photos for her portfolio."

"That's nice."

"It is, but it was nice talking to you. I'm gonna go see what my husband is up to." I smiled.

"Nice talking to you too."

"Hey, is that Uncle Larry?" Nora asked, making my heart stop.

When I saw him pulling up in his cocaine white Rolls Royce, I swallowed a lump in my throat that I didn't even know formed so quickly. When he got out of his car, I went to the passenger side, opening the door.

"Who the fuck is that?" Nora asked with a raised eyebrow, watching our uncle escort a woman that looked around my age out of the car.

"Is that y'all uncle?" Jessica asked.

"Yeah, Uncle Larry. He's an entrepreneur. The richest mother fucker in our family. Shit, he richer than me," Nora replied.

"Well, if it ain't my beautiful nieces. Give Uncle Larry a hug." He smiled, messaging his salt and pepper goatee, looking over at me.

I felt as if I were glued to the spot I was standing in because I couldn't move even if I wanted to. Hearing my son call my name, I turned around and quickly rushed off to him, thanking God for a moment that provided me with a chance to leave.

"What's wrong, Tyreke?" I asked, noticing the mug on his face.

"Where's Star?"

"Upstairs sleeping, why?"

"She has my phone."

"Okay, go upstairs and get it. Check her jacket pocket, but don't wake her up."

"I won't," he replied, running off.

Looking around, making sure I wasn't being watched, I rushed inside the house, making my way upstairs. Since no one was ever on the top floor, I locked myself in the bathroom, pulling out my flask filled with whisky. Unscrewing the top, I threw it back, downing it like it didn't burn the back of my throat like fire.

"Hey Syaire, love, are you in here?" asked Todd, knocking on the door, making me jump.

"Yeah, honey, I just needed a break from all the noise."

"Are you okay, love?"

"Yes, I'm fine. I just need some privacy."

"Okay, well, I'll be downstairs if you need me. You ran off pretty fast, and I was worried."

"I'm fine, honey, I promise. I told you I needed some privacy."

"Okay, well, some more of your family members are pulling up. Your Uncle Larry was asking about you. He said he didn't get a chance to speak to you. You ran off so fast."

"Fuck, Todd! I said I need some fucking privacy. I don't give a fuck about what anybody said! Can you do me this one fucking favor and leave me alone!" I yelled.

When I heard him clear his throat and his footsteps dispersing, I took my flask to the head once again, blinking away my tears.

Chapter 6

ALL I NEEDED

One Day Before Thanksgiving

Tell you what I'm grinding for
Just to see you smile more
Lately I spend all my time
Tryna keep you satisfied
If I can have you all to me
Then I am yours for you to keep
Bring your body close to mine

I hummed the lyrics to Syd's song "Smile More" as I tried to come down from the high that I was on. While Jessica was taking a nap on the ride here, I snorted a line just to take the edge off. It was as if I was becoming addicted to it more and more. It felt as if I was relying on it to make me feel better and make me turn into a different person, which was exactly what I needed. I needed to be the person my family thought I was.

I was so high and jittery that I had to come into my old bedroom just to get some type of privacy. Marley was too busy flirting with Jessica, and Jessica was too busy eyeing down the food that was coming off the grill. Since she was occupied by my family, I finally had time to relax and calm my nerves.

"So you just gonna come through all these people and not say anything to me?"

I looked up from scrolling through my Instagram to see Adrian standing at my door with a plate of ribs and mac n cheese in his hand.

"Hi, I didn't' know you were here. I'm shocked you're here."

"I texted you."

"I haven't been around my phone lately."

"Your face was just all in your phone Nora."

"I'm talking about then."

"Yeah, right."

"That plate must be for me."

"It is," he replied, passing it to me. I sat it on my dresser before walking into Adrian's arms, giving him a hug.

"I was worried about you. You haven't texted me nor called me in weeks."

"I couldn't."

"What did I tell you about that, Nora." He sighed, running his hands down his face.

"I can't leave him, okay. It's not that easy."

"It's not that easy?" he scoffed in disbelief.

"It's not, and you know that."

"I told you, I have the money to get you out of that situation. Nora, I can't sit back and let that shit happen to you. I know how it feels to be stuck in a situation you want so badly to get out of."

"You don't know shit about my situation Adrian."

"Yes, I do. I know everything about your situation. Don't forget who was there for you when your ass almost tried to kill yourself. I've always been there for you, and you know that. You stop accepting money from me, and you're ignoring me and Tru's calls. What's been going on with you?"

"Nothing."

"Stop lying to me," he demanded, fed up trying to keep his composure.

"I'm not taking you or my sister's money because he's going

to do nothing but take it from me. The money you use to send me, I saved up just for this day. I needed it to buy that limo and these clothes."

"When are you gonna stop pretending? You're not this damn huge superstar model you used to be. Your little Nora from Charleston, South Carolina who always had a good head on her shoulders. Come on, man, you gotta tell your parents what's going on."

"If I tell my parents what's going on, you gotta tell Tru why you were in LA a few months ago," I countered, licking my lips and caressing his cheek.

Adrian grabbed my hand, gripping it, pulling it away from his face.

"I was there to help you."

"Yeah, help fuck me to sleep." I scoffed, trying to walk away, but he grabbed me by my face, making me look into his eyes.

"You back on that shit?"

"What?" I asked, confused.

"Are you back on that shit!" he semi-yelled, through gritted teeth.

"And if I was?"

"I can't believe you. I fly out to LA to get you clean and help you get better, and here you are, back at square one."

"Don't you fucking judge me! Don't you dare judge me!"

"What do you expect me to do?"

"Be there for me! You were just like me! You were hooked on drugs just like me! You know how it feels to be strung out and need it! That's how I feel. When I can't feel comfort from anyone or anything else, that's the only thing that keeps me sane."

"I can't be there for you if you don't want me there! You always shut me out."

"Because I can't have you!"

"You know we can't do that. Tru is my life. I can't hurt her."

"You fucked her little sister, so I'm pretty sure we done hurt her. She just doesn't know that," I sarcastically replied, pacing the floor.

"Just like I was there for you to help you get clean, Tru was there for me to help me get clean. I love that girl to death. She's the mother of my child, and she's my wife."

"Now she's your wife."

"Tru—"

"Tru my fucking ass, fuck Tru. You don't love her. You love me. You even told me you loved me, Adrian. If you love me so fucking bad, take me away from what's waiting for me in LA. You know what I go through. You know my pain. I ask you this all the time, and you do nothing but get my fucking hopes up. Don't lie to me. That's all I ask you to do is to not lie to me. Do you love me?"

"Nora, I—"

"Do you fucking love me, Adrian?" I asked, once more stepping to him. He looked hesitant at first before sighing and pulling me back into his chest.

"I love you." He sighed, rubbing circles in my back.

"Prove it."

"Nora, can I talk to you for a second?" Jessica interrupted, making Adrian and I jump.

"Yeah," I replied, watching Adrian walk out.

Jessica closed and locked my room door before coming up to me. I automatically flinched when I saw her about to slap me, but she stopped herself.

"Are you fucking serious? I should beat your ass right now. Your sister's husband? Your fucking your sister's husband," she ranted, pacing the floor, pounding her fist together.

"Mind your business."

"First of all, bitch, you brought me down here to this country ass place to pretend and be your damn assistant when I'm your best friend. Let me repeat that. I'm your best friend, and I would never steer you in the wrong direction. You fucking your sister's husband, and you know you're wrong, Nora."

"What all did you hear?" I asked, hoping she didn't hear about me doing drugs.

I couldn't care less about her finding out about Adrian and me because Jessica was respectful enough to respect my privacy and let me handle a situation like that on my own. I know she would chew me out, but I didn't care. Adrian and I first started talking when I turned eighteen. It was friendly conversation, and he always gave me good advice and kept me on my toes. He even helped me get into the school I wanted to go to in the first place. He was like a mentor at first. When he saw me in LA, I was off my shit, and he knew I was zooted. He helped me get better, and he even paid for rehab. After I got clean, we bonded, and one thing led to another. I couldn't help the feelings I had for him. And I knew he felt the same way about me, regardless of if he was married to my sister or not.

"Just the part that your fucking your sister's husband, bitch?"

"Look, I don't have time for you to judge me."

"Well, I'm about to judge you, bitch."

"Look, you can go back to LA if you're gonna do that the entire trip. I bought you here for support, not to add onto my depression."

"You know what? I'm gonna let you do you. You never listen anyway. When it comes back to bite you in your ass, or in your case, when your sister beat your ass, I'm gonna sit on the sideline and watch her give your ass that work. You're wrong, and you know you're wrong. I'm gonna go mingle with your family and keep up this fake persona shit you got going on. I'll see you later, boss." she replied, walking out of my room, leaving the door open.

"Well, well, well, if it isn't Superstar," my Aunt Jamie taunted, tooting her nose up at me.

"What are you doing up here?"

"I can't come up here and see you. I haven't seen you since you dropped out of college to go and do that lil modeling thing in LA."

"Oh wow, I haven't seen you since your fourth or fifth wedding. Hopefully, this man stays. We both know you get around." I laughed with pettiness laced in it, watching her devious smile turn into a look of disgust.

"Hm, funny. I haven't seen anything in the magazines about you lately. I say your name to certain people, and they don't even know who you are."

"Hm, you know what else is funny. That fake ass wedding ring on your finger. I know you got it out of the jewelry section from TJ Maxx. This husband must not be as rich as the last one."

"This is 14 karats. This shit cost more than your life."

"Bye, Aunt Jamie."

"Bye, Nora," she scoffed, walking out.

"Damn girl, you must have butt-dialed a nigga because that ass is calling me," Marley flirted, following Jessica.

"Nora, get your brother." she groaned, trying to run from him.

This was gonna be one long ass trip. The holidays couldn't get any closer to an end.

Chapter 7:

SO SICK OF LOVE

Tru

"Oh my god, I remember that!" my mother exclaimed.

We were all sitting around the fire in the backyard. Once all the kids were sleeping, the adults decided to get some time to reminisce on things and spend more time together.

"Yeah, so as we all know, Thanksgiving is tomorrow. I was thinking about fixing a few plates to take over to the church tomorrow night. Anybody wanna help me cook extra food?" my mother asked.

"Extra food? Tiffany, we got a whole village over here to feed, and you tryna feed the homeless. Ain't nobody got time for that. You do this every year," my Uncle Lewis complained.

"Lewis, just like you said, I do this every year. I'm thankful enough to feed my family and other people."

"Whatever, I know I'm not cooking extra food for nobody."

"Ain't nobody asked you to. I said if anybody wanted to help, they could. I ain't say, Lewis can you help me cook."

"Mhmm, whatever, Tiffany."

"Has anybody seen Syaire? When I pulled up, she ran off somewhere, and I ain't seen her all day," my Uncle Larry explained.

I scoffed and shook my head at him. Growing up, I never liked him because he always seemed off to me. Even as a child, I never felt comfortable around him. His presence alone made me want to walk away to keep from putting my hands on him. Before

I could respond to his question, Todd beat me to it.

"She wasn't feeling well, so she decided to call it a night early."

"Oh wow, maybe I'll catch her tomorrow," he replied, rubbing on his girlfriend's thigh as she sat on his lap.

"May I be excused?" I asked my mother and father, as if I was still a child. I cursed my manners sometimes.

"Why?" asked my mother.

"You're fine, go ahead, sweetheart," my father chimed in, making my mother give him the side-eye.

Getting up from my seat, I went inside and headed straight toward my bedroom. As soon as I was about to open my room door, I heard my name being called. Turning around, I smiled, seeing my little brother, Montray.

"Oh my god, when did you get in?" I asked, bringing him into a hug.

"I just got here."

"Oh wow, everybody's in the backyard. Why didn't you come out?"

"Because I was looking for you."

"Well, you found me, little brother. What's going on?"

He looked over to his guest before clearing his throat.

"Tell her?" his guest urged.

"Uh, no disrespect, but who are you?"

"Oh my bad, Tru, this is my best friend, Darius. Darius, this is my big sister Tru."

"Nice to meet you, Darius."

"Likewise."

"Can we talk somewhere private?" Montray asked.

I could tell by how nervous he was that it was something serious. Since our rooms were right down the hall from one another, we went to his bedroom. Montray was the middle child out of the six of my siblings. He attended Morehouse, and he was the one who always made my parents the proudest. He sang in the church choir and school choir, played football, and got a full ride to college. Montray attended church every Sunday and was the first to wake up every morning, and he graduated from high school at the top of his class. He was the golden boy, and my parents made that known.

Once we were inside his room, he closed the door behind him.

"What's going on?" I asked, sitting down beside him on his twin bed.

"I don't know how to say this?"

"Say what? Please don't tell me you knocked somebody up." I sighed.

"No, it's not that."

"Okay, speak to me."

"I think I fucked up."

"You fucked up for doing something that makes you happy?" Darius scoffed.

"Hey, can you step outside for me real quick so I can talk to my brother?"

"I think I should be here when he tells you."

"It's fine, Darius. Can you give us a sec, please?"

"Okay, I'll be right outside the door." Darius sighed, walking out and shutting the door behind him.

"Now talk to me, come on, Tray, we tell each other everything. You, Kyle, and Marley are the only ones I really kept in touch with."

"I think mom and dad are gonna be pissed with it. You know how they are when it comes to this."

"Stop beating around the bush and tell me. You know I won't judge you. Unlike Nora and Syaire, I'm the big sister that's going to listen to you."

"I'm gay."

"What?"

"I'm gay," he repeated himself, this time smiling and letting out a deep sigh.

"Your gay?"

"Yes, Tru, I'm gay."

"When did you find out that you were?"

"My freshman year of college."

"Montray, you're a junior now. When were you going to tell me? When were you going to tell mama and daddy?"

"I didn't think it was the right time, and it still isn't the right time."

"Okay, so how did you know from the jump that you were gay?"

"I was invited to a strip club by my friend Taz. I didn't know it was a gay strip club until we pulled up. I mean, she always brought me to certain events that supported the LGBTQ community, and me being a supportive friend, I went. I guess being around all that for three years helped me figure out the real me."

"The real you? Look, Montray deciding that you wanna be gay is a big decision. Of course, baby brother, I support you either way, but being around that community doesn't make you turn gay. I understand if you're confused, bu—"

"I'm not confused, Tru."

"Who all knows about this?"

"Just Taz, Darius, and now you."

"And what did Darius say."

"Darius is my boyfriend."

"Your boyfriend? Oh, sweet Jesus." I sighed, getting up pacing the floor.

"What?"

"You invited your boyfriend here, around your religious mother who doesn't know that you're gay. You know she's gonna freak out, right?"

"That's why I'm coming to you for help. What do you think I should do?"

"I think you should tell the truth."

"What if they hate me? What if they disown me? What if—"

"Stop thinking about the what-if's and think about the relief it's going to bring you. You see how this family treats me and how they see me, and I don't care. It took a lot for me to come here for the holidays, Montray. If I'm living past the judgment, I think you can too."

"So when should I tell them?"

"Tomorrow on Thanksgiving, or the day after. At least on Thanksgiving, you can tell the entire family, and they can hopefully be supportive. I mean, you know Uncle Lewis is homophobic as fuck, so you know for a fact that he's gonna judge you. Still, I wouldn't care about what Uncle Lewis says because his ass had to get his leg amputated for drinking so damn much. So he can't judge anybody."

"Your right." He laughed lightly.

"I know I am, so lighten up and prepare yourself to tell them. I'll be here holding your hand the entire time."

"Thank you. I love you so much, Tru."

"I love you too, Tray. I'm gonna check on my daughter. Just

remember what I said."

"I will."

I gave him a hug before walking out. Before heading to my room, I stopped and looked over at Darius.

"Take care of my brother."

"I always will."

"Good."

Going into my bedroom, I saw Royal was still knocked out. When I saw Adrian deep in his phone, I knocked on the door frame, alerting him, causing him to look up.

"Hey, I didn't see you," he said, putting his phone face down on the dresser.

"Yeah, I noticed. What was that?"

"What was what?"

"You don't never put your phone face down when I walk in the room. What's going on with you?" I asked, coming in and closing the door.

"Damn, if you must know, I'm checking to see when your gift is coming in. I had to change the address for here since we were going to be here for the holidays."

"Oh wow, so what did you get me?" I smiled, walking over to him like a big kid and sitting on his lap.

"Ha, real funny. You know I can't tell you."

"Mhm, whatever. So, I was thinking…."

"Thinking what?"

"That maybe we take Royal to Marley's room or Nora's room for the night, and we have some alone time." I smiled, pecking his lips and tugging at his chin hair.

"Eh."

"Eh? Eh, what?"

"I'm not up for it tonight."

"Wow!" I replied in defeat.

"Wow, what?"

"Lately, you're never up for it. What's going on? Are you good?"

"I'm straight."

"It doesn't look like it. Lately, you haven't been touching me, and you barely wanna kiss me? Adrian, that's not like you."

"I just haven't been in the mood baby, it's not you."

"Yeah, whatever, goodnight," I replied, trying to walk off, but he grabbed my arm, pulling me back in his lap.

"Don't is that."

"Do what?"

I sighed, just wanting to go somewhere to cry. It was always like me to think the worse, and my anxiety was the blame for that. *What if he didn't love me anymore? Am I unattractive to him now? What if he was cheating on me?* My mind was bustling with questions.

"Be mad at me and overthink. I know how you are, Tru."

"I'm fine."

"No, you're not." I sighed.

"I said I'm fine. Let's leave it at that, Adrian."

"Okay, then give me a kiss."

"No, you ain't been wanting my lips on you lately, so don't ask for a kiss just because you feel like you fucked up."

"What you mean I fucked up? I just want a kiss from my wife."

"You want a kiss, okay."

I pecked his cheek before jumping out of his lap and walking off.

"Real mature!" he yelled.

Ignoring him, I went downstairs at sat on the front porch, letting the cool November breeze brush against my skin. I only had on a pair of sweatpants and a tank top. I forgot how bipolar the weather in South Carolina could get. During the day, it could be cold, and at night it could be hot. Sometimes it would be the other way around.

Since everyone was in the backyard, I found some type of privacy sitting in the front. That was one thing I could never get was privacy in this house with all my family members under the same roof.

"I knew that face looked familiar."

Looking up, I was face-to-face with my old friend, Hasaun. Hasaun and I grew up together, and after I up and left for Florida, I lost all communication with him. I lost all contact with everyone. Hasaun wasn't just an old friend. He was an old boyfriend.

"Oh my god. Hasaun, is that you?" I smiled, getting up embracing him into a hug.

"In the flesh."

"Wow, it's been years."

"Who you tellin'." He smiled.

"What you doing here? I thought you moved to Charlotte."

"I did, but I decided to move back to be closer to my son."

"Oh my god, you have a son?

Yeah, he's six."

"So is my daughter."

"You got a daughter?"

"Yeah, damn, it's been a while."

"I know, shit I thought you done forgot about a nigga."

"I did, I'm not gonna lie."

"Damn, that's fucked up. We were tight. I ain't gonna lie when you left, you had me feeling some type of way. Then you changed your number, so you had me thinking I did something wrong."

"I just was going through a lot back then. I needed a fresh start."

"There's nothing wrong with that, but you could have at least given a nigga the heads-up."

"I know, and I'm sorry."

"But how you been, though?"

"I've been good. What you doing here, though?"

"Your mom invited me over."

"She did?" I replied with a raised eyebrow with confusion written all over my face. My mother wasn't a huge fan of Hasaun and for her to invite him over was off to me.

"Yeah, she did."

"Oh, okay."

"Is there a problem with that?"

"No, there's no problem. It's just you know how my mom is. I just found it weird that she invited you over."

"I did too, but my mom wanted to grab a plate from over here, so that's another reason I came."

"Oh, okay, how's your mother?"

"She's good. I don't know if you knew or not, but she finally beat her cancer."

"Oh my god, that's great! I'm happy for her."

"Yeah, I'm happy she's better too. You know how close my mama and me are."

"I know."

"Hey, you wanna go for a walk and catch up?"

"I don't know. It's getting late."

"Oh yeah, you probably wanna get back to your daughter. My bad, it was just a suggestion."

"She's up there with my husband."

"You're married?"

"Yeah, I am."

"That's wassup."

"Yeah, he's a good man."

"He better be. If he fucks up, I'll fuck him up. You know you're my best friend." He smiled, nudging my shoulder.

"I know." I laughed, trying to hide my cheeks from turning rosy red.

"Man, come on, walk with me. I need to know what the hell you've been up to," Hasaun urged, placing his hand out, pulling me up off the step. Looking hesitant at first at my bedroom window, I sighed before agreeing to walk with him.

We spent two hours conversing and about any and everything.

Chapter 8

WHERE DID WE GO WRONG

Thanksgiving Day

"What's been going on with you?" Todd quizzed, fixing his tie in the full body mirror.

"Nothing."

"It's been something. What's wrong? I know when something is bothering you, Syaire."

"Todd, can you please leave it alone? Honey, I said I'm fine. Come on, it's Thanksgiving, and we need to get down there and help my family set everything up."

"I know, but still, I'm worried about you."

"Okay, and for what? I don't know why. You need to stop all that worrying before your blood pressure goes up."

"Ever since we got here, you've been acting a little off, Sy."

"I'll be downstairs. I said I'm fine," I insisted, walking off.

Amid walking downstairs, I bumped into my Uncle Larry, who was still in his Versace robe. When I was trying to walk off, he grabbed me.

"Get your fucking hands off of me!" I yelled.

"Okay, okay, I'm sorry," he replied, putting his hands up in surrender.

"Don't you ever touch me again!"

"Why have you been so distant, Syaire? We family, I used to

be your favorite uncle."

"Favorite uncle? After what you did to me."

"Don't start with that bullshit again. Syaire, I'm your uncle. I would never do anything to hurt you."

"You raped me! You came into my room every night and raped me when I was only ten! What do you call that, huh?" I yelled in his face.

"I would never touch you or look at you in that way. Syaire, it was probably a nightmare. You don't know what you're saying."

"Yes, I do know what the fuck I'm saying. You came into my room, touched me, and told me if I told anyone that you would hurt Tru next. Don't sit here and lie to me, I know what you did to me every night, and you know it too. If I catch you around my kids, I will kill you, and I want you to know that. Don't come near me again," I warned, walking off, drying the tears I never knew that fell.

As if it were just my luck, before I could make it down to the kitchen completely, Tru stopped me.

"What was all that about?" she quizzed.

"All what?" I sighed, completely tired of everyone asking me the same question.

"I heard your conversation with Uncle Larry."

"Ok, so?"

"So, when were you going to tell mama and daddy? Shit, tell me or anyone. Does Todd know?"

"Nobody needs to know shit. I've been keeping it a secret for this long, so let's leave it at that. No one would believe me."

"I believe."

"Oh, Tru, fuck you. Stop tryna kiss ass."

"Kiss ass? I just found out that my uncle raped my big sister, and I'm kissing ass? I'm trying to help you."

"Help me? Oh, baby sister, you could never help me. I got me. Do me a favor and stay out of my business."

"You know what? I try to hold my tongue with you because I know how you get sometimes, but you need to really chill out."

"You know what you need to know? You need to open your fucking eyes and see what's going on in your relationship. Adrian isn't the man you think he is, sweetheart. This lil front that you putting on for the entire family may work for them, but it ain't working for me. You know these walls are thin, Aunt Jamie's mouth is as big as the goddamn ocean. Your man ain't fuck you in months, and you got the nerve to be on some lil girl high school shit, taking long walks with your ex and not coming into the house until two in the morning. Girl, get your shit together and worry about the business that pays you."

"You know what? Fuck you. You think you know so fucking much, but you don't know shit about what I'm going through and what I been through. I was gonna let that shit you just said slide, but I'm not. Did you tell Todd your drinking? You smell like a goddamn fish. The Colgate ain't working because I still smell the alcohol on your breath. Stay out of my marriage, and I'll stay out of yours. Don't say shit to me the entire trip that I'm here because all I ever did was try to be a good little sister to you and make sure you were straight, but you always treat me like you hate me. So treat me the same way because after this shit is over, we won't be speaking after just like it was before," Tru replied, leaving me there looking dumbfounded.

Tru never stood up to me the way she did. I could do nothing but sit there in shock at the way she just talked to me.

"Damn, she told you," Nora said, walking past me.

"Oh, bitch fuck you? You think I don't know about you?" I replied, shaking my head, ready to bring all the bullshit to the table. I was still a little tipsy from the whole bottle of Jack Daniels that I drunk early this morning, and the mood I was in, anybody could have got this work.

"Oh no, just because Tru piss in your cereal this morning, don't try and bring that shit to me. I ain't do nothing to you."

"You ain't do shit but lie."

"Lie? Lie?! What the hell did I lie about?"

"Maybe you should watch how you talk to your assistant, or should I say best friend. Maybe if your lips weren't so busy sucking your sister's husband's dick, you would know that your best friend left last night. Just like I told Tru, these walls are thin. I heard the little argument you had last night with her. Bitch, I know that you're broke, you're being pimped out by your ex-boyfriend's friend, and that you're not living as lavish as you are making people think. The next time you wanna try to add your two cents to some shit, make sure you have two pennies to rub together bitch," I sneered, bumping her shoulder, leaving Nora there looking dumbfounded.

When I got to the kitchen, I put on my best face and helped my mother and aunties put things together. I didn't give a fuck how Nora nor Tru felt about how I read their asses. Ever since I got here, I wasn't feeling myself, and I'll be damn if I was gonna be like that the entire trip. I felt as if when I was drunk, I was now the same person I became when I was in Tennessee. I was Syaire mother fucking Nelson, and I was gonna make that known. I wasn't gonna let my whack ass family see me struggle or down.

Even if that meant hiring someone to take Uncle Larry out, shit, I had the money. Ever since I was little, he ruined my life. I still lived with what he did to me, and that was the reason I drank. Before I met Todd, I used to smoke cigarettes and weed to get my mind off it. After I helped him recover from being an alcoholic, I wanted to try that mechanism myself to see if it would numb the pain, and it did just that. I kept what Uncle Larry did to me a secret for years because he threatened to hurt Tru. Hating to admit it, that was the reason I held some type of hate for her. When I was younger, I actually told Tru what happened. She was a quiet child, so I knew she wouldn't run and tell our parents. She was too young to understand as well, and I hated that. I wanted her to tell, I wanted her to help me because I couldn't help myself.

I still had love for my little sister. I really did. The thing was, I envied her. I envied that she never let what my family said or think bother her. I envied her perfect, thriving career. Shit, I even used to envy having a husband like hers until I found out that he was fucking Nora. At times I just wondered where I went wrong?

Chapter 9:

SILENT CRIES

While everyone was sitting at the dinner table laughing it up and conversing about the old and the new, I sat there spaced out. It was one thing for Jessica to know that Adrian and I were messing around, but it was another thing for my loud mouth, bougie, ass sister to find that out. I already know her and Tru aren't the best of friends either and that she would throw that in her face in a heartbeat. I didn't even know she heard the argument between Jessica and me last night. Shit, I didn't even know Jessica up and left last night. I was just oblivious to everything. I didn't even care that I knew about Syaire becoming an alcoholic. It's the fact that my secret is way bigger than hers. I felt as if I was losing everyone who I was close with.

I snapped on Marley for coming at me sideways about Jessica, Syaire and I were throwing daggers at one another, and I've been distancing myself away from family more. I could tell what Adrian and I were doing was really fucking with Tru. Adrian has been sneaking in my room at three in the morning for the past few days we were here. I could even hear him and Tru arguing at times, and part of me felt sorry for doing what I was doing, but I loved him, and he loved me.

For once, I actually felt happy with everything crazy going on in my life, and I'll be damned if I sit there and let anybody ruin it, even Tru. Shit, even if that meant cutting Jessica off, I could live with that. Call it selfish, but sometimes you have to be selfish to maintain your happiness. Jessica was my ride or die, and she was always there when I needed her, but last night was more explosive between her and me than it has ever gotten.

Last Night

"*You fucking serious right now!*" she yelled, knocking the little bit of coke that I had on my nails off.

"*Don't you fucking judge me! Don't you dare judge me!*" I said, half out of it.

Adrian and I had got into a huge argument about how he couldn't keep doing what we were doing. The way he expressed his love for Tru really hurt me to the core because that's how I wanted him to feel about me. I was on edge, and I needed something to get me straight. During that time, Jessica was actually entertaining Marley's ass, and I thought he had her occupied. Shit, she was even sleeping in his room. The way Marley bragged about fucking bitches, he would have been told me that he was fucking Jessica. I guess she was giving him good conversation and company, and he liked that. Shit, she even told me he was good at keeping conversation. I knew they were hitting it off because they both enjoyed basketball, and they bonded over that, just like that.

"*How long have you been doing this shit?*" Jess asked, trying to calm down.

"*Why does it matter?*"

"*Bitch, you're doing drugs! What do you mean, why does it matter? What the hell is going on with you?!*" she yelled, pushing me.

"*Woah, hold up, you put your hand on me one more time, and I will fuck you up, Jess.*"

"*Go ahead and do it. Where is the rest of it?*" she demanded, rummaging through my room, knocking shit off shelves.

"*It's all gone.*" I laughed, wiping the tip of my nose and sitting on my bed, laying back.

"*You know what? Since you don't wanna take me seriously. I'll go tell your parents,*" she warned about to walk out. As fast as I sniffed that coke, was as quickly as I got up and jumped on her ass.

"You're not telling my parents shit. Who the fuck do you think you are, storming up in here telling me what I should and shouldn't do? This is my fucking body!"

"Is life really that fucking hard for you? Did Samson really hurt you that bad to have you hooked on crack? To have you fucking your sister's husband. Are you doing this because your career is nonexistent? You need to grow the fuck up, Nora. Your wrong, and you know you wrong. And one thing I won't do is sit here and let my best friend be hook on drugs. Get your shit together and get it together now because I'm not here to sit back and watch your ruin yourself."

"You know what? Fuck you! Leave, I don't need you. I don't need anyone. Get out! Don't your fucking grandma got cancer and you here in South Carolina fucking on my lil brother? By the time you head back home, your grandmother might be in a body bag. Your su—"

I was cut off by her punching me in my face, causing me to fumble back in the wall. I held my nose that was throbbing, but it didn't even hurt. I got my ass beat every day, and this shit was like a breeze to me. Getting back up, I ran up on her, and she grabbed me by my hair, slinging me on the floor.

"You must have forgotten that I used to beat bitches bloody. I'm from Inglewood, bitch. Don't play with me. I don't know what y'all do here in South Carolina, baby, but I'm not about to let you run up on me. I find it funny that you could run up on me and try to beat my ass, but you couldn't raise your hand to Samson. And I know I'm a shitty person for leading my sick grandmother back home, to be here and support my best friend's bullshit ass lie. You want me to leave, I'm out. Fuck you! Don't call me when he has your ass on the corner selling pussy to pay for rent. Happy Thanksgiving," she said, grabbing her purse and running out the door.

"Nora, did you hear me? Where's your assistant friend?" my mother asked, knocking me from my thoughts.

"She had to leave early."

"For what reason? She was a nice girl. We really enjoyed her company. I wish she would have said goodbye first."

"She had a problem back home, so she had to leave, mom. I'll tell her you guys enjoyed her visit."

"Are you serious right now?" Marley scoffed, shaking his head at me.

Ignoring him, I rolled my eyes. I didn't care how mad he was at me. He should have never been in ear hustling in the first place. He was mad for all the wrong reasons at that. He didn't care about how Jess talked to me. All he cared about was the girl he was feeling just left.

"Anyway, does anyone wanna bless the food?" my father asked, clearing his throat.

"I'd like to," Marley offered, causing everyone to side-eye him. It wasn't like Marley to bless the food because he was always the first to slip a piece of food in his mouth.

Marley let out a deep chuckle, which worried me. He always had this sadistic laugh when he had something he wanted to get off his mind, and the last thing we needed was him blurting my business out in front of the entire family.

"No, I'll bless it."

"First of all, neither of y'all ever like saying grace, now the both of you wanna say it. Hell must be about to freeze over," Aunt Jamie chimed in, taking a sip of her wine.

"Who you tellin'," my father added, letting out a light laugh.

"I think I should do it. Let's bow our heads," Marley said.

"No, I said I was doing it."

"How about the both of you do it," my Aunt Carrissa suggested, fed up with our bickering.

"I don't care who does it. I prefer my baby Montray do it," my grandmother on my father's side spoke up.

"Dear heavenly father, I wanna thank you for bringing my family together to have yet another beautiful Thanksgiving. Bless the hands that prepared this food and bless the minds, bodies, and souls that are about to endure it. In God's name am—"

Marley interrupted my Aunt Jolene, making me open my eyes as quickly as they closed. Aunt Jolene was my grandmother's sister. Of course, her old ass would wanna say grace. She acts like we didn't know she was outside smoking a pound of weed with my cousins. It doesn't matter that her weed was prescribed. She was still smoking that good shit that came off the street. We all knew she was high and had the munchies. She wasn't fooling nobody, saying grace all holy like and shit.

"Dear Lord, before Aunt Jolene's high ass ends the prayer, I just wanna say thank you for bringing most of my siblings home for Thanksgiving. I know we're missing our big brother Kyle, but we pray that you bring him home safely for us tomorrow morning, so we can not only spend Christmas but New Year's Day with him as well."

"Amen, can we eat?" my nephew Tyreke asked, with mostly sweet potato pie and cupcakes on his plate.

"Shut up, finish your prayer, Uncle Marley." Star smiled.

"God, you know family is really something else," Marley continued.

"Oh Lord, here we go," Montray mumbled.

"Lord, the family you bless me with have been nothing but kind, amazing, truthful, and loving."

"Yes God, preach, nephew," urged my religious ass Aunt Chrissy. Auntie Chrissy was a pastor, and she always went overboard when it came time to pray.

"Lord, that is what I would say if it was true. Lord, please make sure when I bite into the rice that Aunt Jamie cooked, I don't swallow one of her fake teeth. Please give Aunt Jamie the common sense to see that not only her third husband but her fourth husband is a faggot, and we know she's only using him for his money. Please God, I beg of you to bless me with better sisters because the sisters I got ain't shit. You must have had your side angel making them when you went on break because something is really wrong with the three sisters you put in my life.

God, you have given me a chance to finally find true love. I see what they mean when they say the devil can be in disguise because Lord knows my hoe ass sister Nora Garrett is definitely rocking them devil horns on her head the same way she rocks that fake ass Gucci dress she gotta return when she goes back to L.A.

Who would have known that not only was my sister a crack head, but she fucking my other sister's husband? Oh Lord, you work in mysterious ways. Let's not forget that she's broke and the nigga she with be pimping her out, and her house got roaches. Oh Lord, please bless my sister with not only a new brain but make sure that brain got common sense. Lord, please put Uncle Lewis' ass back in jail for six months because he doesn't understand that these young ass girls' parents will have his ass walking on two nubs instead of one. He claims his leg was amputated because he was an alcoholic, but we all know he got shot in the leg for fucking with his new girlfriend's twenty-three-year-old daughter. We all knew that shotgun blew his ass away, damn near blew his muffin cap back blue.

Lord please, bring my Uncle Larry's young fine thang right my way because we both know she's using him for his money. We all know she doesn't want his old ass, God you got a lot of work to do on my family becau—"

"Marley!" my mother and father yelled at the same time.

"Oh, shit," my Uncle Lewis mumbled, slouching down in his seat.

"Damn, that's cold." Syaire laughed, taking a sip of her water.

"You know what? You would be the one to say something."

I laughed maniacally, shaking my head.

"Yup and did. Marley's telling the truth. You are nothing but a broke, lazy, coke head, ass hoe."

"And bitch you ain't nothing but a fucking alcoholic who flaunts shit that you don't have. I feel sorry that Todd has to sleep next to your drunk, sleazy, bougie ass."

"Ain't nothing wrong with being bougie, baby," Aunt Jamie chimed in.

"Shut the fuck up, Jamie, and worry about what's goin' on in your life. Ain't your husband fucking your gym trainer?" my Aunt Carrissa accused.

"And ain't you fucking your boyfriend's son? Hm, might have to trade that five-dollar clearance rack Citi Trends ass Dashiki in for an orange jumpsuit soon. Ain't he like sixteen?"

"You know what, Nora? Fuck you! Girl, I will get up and beat your ass." Syaire threatened, taking off her hoops.

"Oh, please do, do it! Beat my ass. Don't fall on your ass. I hope you not drunk when you stand up."

"Syaire, you're drinking?" Todd asked with hurt written all over his face.

"Did you tell Tru yet?" Syaire asked, making me swallow the lump in my throat. It was just like her to ignore her husband and try to take the attention away from her.

"Tell me what?" Tru asked, looking over at me.

"Hey baby, I think we need to get up and talk."

"Oh no, don't get up and walk away now, ese. Don't walk away now. Tell my sister the truth," Marley demanded, sticking a spoon full of rice and cabbage in his mouth.

"Come on, Superstar, your front and center, tell her," Syaire egged on.

Sadly she was right, and all I could do was look to Adrian for some type of support, but he looked as nervous as I was. I picked up my glass of water before taking a sip.

"Nora, what are they talking about?" my mother questioned. Tru just sat there with the same question written on her face.

"Shit, y'all can't put it together. Tru she fucking your novio nigga," Marley revealed. Tru's chest did nothing but heave up and down, and she sat there staring at me.

"Is it true?" she asked me.

"Yes."

"Hm, you're a bitch. You are such a fucking bitch, and Adrian, I should have known. I should have fucking known, but I guess I was too blinded by love. You're fucking my little sister. I can't believe you."

"Shit, I can. I told you from day one I didn't like his Spanish looking ass," Syaire chimed in.

"How about you stay the fuck out of this and worry about your alcohol problem and how your gonna handle that with Todd," Tru clapped back at Syaire.

"Oh, bitch please," Syaire sneered, scrunching her nose up at her.

"Stop it, Syaire. She's right. We need to talk," Todd said.

"No, we don't."

"Yes, we do!" he yelled, slamming his fist on the table, making everyone jump.

"Oh shit, white man done got mad. Let me get my food and leave," Marley announced, getting up from the table with his plate and a whole pitcher of Kool-Aid, heading up to his room. Yes, the entire pitcher of Kool-Aid.

"I can't believe you, Sy. How could you help me with my addiction and turn around and make it your own? Your such a hypocrite.”

“Todd—”

“Don't Todd me,” he said, getting up from the table and walking off. I saw nothing but rage filling Syaire's eyes as she looked over at Tru with the same anger. If looks could kill, this entire house would be a murder scene.

“See what you did. This is why I never fucking liked being around you. You always stick your nose in business that doesn't mind you. You do know that barely anyone wanted you here, right? Mama didn't want you here, I didn't want you here, everybody fucking hates you because you always thought you were better than everyone else. You were always so fucking stuck up and never kept in touch with anyone, and you have the nerve to come here and pretend that your marriage and your life is so fucking perfect when it isn't.

You think you could just up and leave and get your fancy new job, travel, and do this that and the third and come back and be with your family when it's most convenient. I've always had love for you Tru, but you're an evil bitch, and I want nothing to do with you. I fucking hate you, I hate your fucking guts, and I wish you were dead. If you went through half the shit that I had to bust my ass and go through, you would fold like any other bitch in these streets. I made sacrifices for you ever since you got into this world, and *you prove and show me every day that it should have been you and never me.*”

“Syaire, that is enough!” my mother yelled.

“No, mama, she wanna cause a scene. Well, I'm about to make the entire fucking movie. You are nothing but a salty bitch, and you show me that every day. You think it bothers me that my relationship with any of you isn't as strong as I want it to be. Cause it doesn't bother me, not one fucking bit. Don't blame me for what happened to you. You need to tell mama and daddy what happened? As a matter of fact, nah, I'll tell them.

Did you all know that Uncle Larry raped her when she was younger? That's why she drinks. She's becoming an alcoholic because of that. She acts like we don't know that she's this broken little girl in a grown woman's body. I know you better than you know yourself. I've tried everything to prove myself to the people in this family, and all I got was the short end of the fucking stick. To mama, I was never holy enough, to daddy, I was never strong enough. To Aunt Jamie, I was never successful enough. To you, Syaire, I was never good enough. Well, from now on, I don't give a fuck about what anybody thinks. I'm out of here," Tru vented, walking away from the table.

"Tru, baby girl, don't do that," my father urged, trying to get up and catch her.

I scoffed, just seeing Adrian run after her as well. I could see the pain in his eyes, and it made me cry. I quickly wiped my tears. It was as if so much was going on that I didn't even see my mother crying, nor did I see Todd rush back in here and put his hands on Uncle Larry. Todd had my Uncle Larry pinned up against the wall.

"I'm gonna kick your ass!" Todd yelled, punching Uncle Larry in the face.

"Todd, let him go!" Syaire yelled.

Before he knew it, my Uncle Larry rushed Todd into a wall so hard that the family portrait dropped. Before anyone could stop her, Syaire busted my Uncle Larry upside the head with a champagne bottle.

"Oh shit, did you kill him?" his girlfriend Keisha yelled.

"I hope I did," replied Syaire going over to check on Todd.

"Damn, what did I miss?" asked Marley, coming down with an empty plate.

"Todd, baby, are you okay?" asked Syaire, checking on him. He was sitting on the floor hyperventilating."

"I think I'm having a heart attack," said Todd, clutching

onto his chest.

"Somebody call 911!" Syaire yelled, making me pull my phone out.

"Oh damn, we all going to jail. This white man is about to croak. I'm too pretty to go to jail, man. I'm not tryna be nobody boyfriend," Marley panicked, pacing the floor.

Chapter 10:

SECRETS UNDER MY TREE

One Week Before Christmas

In my mind, I want you to be free
For all of our friends
To listen to me
Now hear what I say
We wish you a Merry Christmas (Merry Christmas)
To each one of you (To all of you)

I woke up to the sound of the Temptations version of Silent Night, as the scent of candy cane Glade candle's aroma lit my nostrils up like the Fourth of July. Looking down, I smiled, seeing hands wrapped around my waist while my daughter slept peacefully on the couch across from the bed. Stirring in my sleep, I turned around to be faced with Hasaun, who was wide away.

"Uh, ew, that was creepy. You've been up the entire time while I was sleeping." I laughed lightly.

"I was. I just miss having you in my arms. I forgot how good it felt."

"Same, you were always comforting to me."

"I'm glad to hear that. You talked to your family yet?"

"Nope, and I won't be."

"So, are you gonna spend time with my family and me for Christmas, if what you're getting at?"

"Maybe, I don't know yet."

"I personally feel as if you need to be with your family for the holidays. I know all that shit that went down on Thanksgiving got you feeling a lil discourage, but sometimes family is all we got. And Kyle picking your daughter up and taking her over there isn't a good look for you."

"I don't care how it looks. I always cared about certain things when it came to my parents and my family. I always try to present myself in a presentable manner, and I guess it took for the holidays to come around for me to realize how fucked up my family is. I just wanna be surrounded by people who actually love me and won't lie to me."

"I know Kyle's happy he missed Thanksgiving."

"Who are you telling. Syaire's husband had a heart attack, she gave my Uncle Larry a concussion, my daddy and my other uncles beat Uncle Larry's ass, Marley fucked Uncle Larry's girlfriend, and Aunt Jamie and Aunt Carrissa fought. Whew, Lord, Thanksgiving was real ratchet. I know for a fact that my mother is pissed off with me. Even after getting half of what I wanted to say off my chest, I still didn't get a chance to tell her how I really felt. But one thing for certain, telling Syaire ass off was the highlight of my night."

"I know." Hasaun laughed lightly.

"Mhm, I'm serious."

"So what are you gonna do about your husband?" he asked, tracing his finger across my wedding band.

"What can I do about him?"

"He cheated on you with Nora. What do you feel like doing, Tru? It's up to you."

"I don't know." I sighed, looking over at Royal.

"Do you still love him?"

"Hasaun, he's my husband. Yes, I still love him."

"Okay, so what you wanna do."

"I just said I don't know." I groaned, burying my face into his chest. He pulled my face up, making me look at him.

"If you still love him, and you know for a fact that those feelings are going anywhere, then go back. I'm speaking to you as your friend, not your ex. Baby girl, I still love you, and you know how hard we rock, but I'm far from a bitter nigga. I love you, and I wanna see you happy. I know you built a relationship with this nigga, and y'all got a child together, so I support whatever decision you make. I'm not justifying his actions either, but people cheat. I mean, certain people cheat. I had to rephrase that."

"But you didn't cheat on me when we were together."

"Because I knew what I had. Apparently, he probably got caught up and didn't know what he had."

"You're right." I sighed.

"Don't look like that."

"I wish I never left. I just wish we stayed together. I always felt so safe and never had to second guess what you did. I thought Adrian was my everything."

"Sometimes, we choose the wrong people."

"What if I'm the wrong person too?" I asked, looking over at Royal. Adrian wasn't the only one harvesting skeleton's in his closet. So was I.

"How you mean?"

"What if I told you something that could possibly ruin our friendship?"

"You know I'm a calm dude, and I'm understanding. What you gotta tell me, you cheated too?"

"I did."

"What?"

"When Adrian was hooked on drugs, he would be so out of it that I felt like I was a babysitter and not a girlfriend to him. I felt as if I was his fucking mother. When I saw you six years ago, and I told you I was single, I lied. I was seeing Adrian at the time."

"Okay, and we were both wasted. Shit, I know for a fact I couldn't see straight, and we both know your ass still a lightweight."

"Royal isn't Adrian's baby."

"What?"

"She's yours," I revealed, hoping for Hasaun not to go crazy on my ass. He just caught me completely off guard when he sat there with this big ass grin on his face.

"I know."

"What? How do you mean, you know?" I asked, getting up, looking at him sideways.

"I know you better than you know yourself, Tru. The only person you trust with your secrets is Montana. Montana told me the second you told her. You know she's my cousin. The only reason I didn't reach out and try to do or say anything was because I knew one way or another, you were going to tell me. It was shitty that it took six years, but I know how to read people. I even knew Adrian was the type of person I thought he was. Any other nigga would have been sick, knowing another man raising his baby. But me, I took what was in your best interest as a thought. Whenever you would send photos to Montana, she would send them to me. I even got photos of Royal when she was a baby."

"Wow."

"I know."

"Why the hell are you so fucking perfect?"

"Tru, nobody's perfect, baby. And that's what I'm trying to get you to understand about your family. As a matter of fact, new topic. What do you want for Christmas? And really think about the question."

"Really? Come on, you know I don't care about gifts."

"Answer the question. What do you want that you know no one can give you but yourself?"

"I want the chance to be myself, I wanna be Tru, the real Tru."

"Then do that for yourself on Christmas. You can be yourself around me, so be yourself around them, and tell Adrian the truth."

"I will."

"Good, and I'll be by your side the entire time."

"Thank you." I smiled, pecking his lips.

Ever since the mayhem that happened on Thanksgiving, I've been staying with Hasaun and his mother for the time being. Whenever Adrian wanted to see Royal, my big brother Kyle came over and got her, and he rotated taking her back and forth. Kyle even respected my privacy by not telling any of the family where I was.

"Silent night! Holy Night!" Ms. Owen yelled, busting in the room with her Christmas robe on and a cup of eggnog in her hand.

"Mama, come on man. It's too early for that, and Royal is sleeping."

"Oh my bad, then get up. I got breakfast ready for everybody." She smiled.

Hasaun looked exactly like his mother down to a T. They shared the same light skin complexion, doe shaped eyes, and narrow noses. Due to his mother just beating cancer, she kept a low cut, and her hair was dyed pink. Even after recovering from cancer and having one of her breasts removed, she looked as young as ever.

"Good morning, Ms. Owen."

"Morning baby, how's Hasaun treating you?"

"He's treating me just fine."

"Just like a taught him," she bragged.

"You taught him well." I smiled.

"I know."

"Good, we'll be down in a few, ma," Hasaun chimed in, trying to kick her out of the room.

"Mhm, I'm going, I'm going. It's not like y'all can do nothing freaky with this baby in this room."

"Ma, ain't' nobody doin' none of that." Hasaun sighed.

"Mhm, and your baby mama is on her way to drop off Hareem."

"Okay, we'll be down in a minute, mama."

"Please don't tell me your baby mama is one of those ratchet ass girls who live on the block."

"Nah, she's not. She's actually cool."

"As in y'all still fucking. Got it." I smiled awkwardly.

"We not fucking."

"I'm sorry, I don't believe that. Every baby daddy still gonna be fucking with they baby mama."

"Well, she's not. She's married and got three other kids now. I think you'll like her. She reminds me of you."

"I don't know whether to be offended or flattered that you compared me to another woman."

"Be both. She's a wedding planner, and she's got her head on straight. You know that ratchet shit never impressed me."

"You're right."

When Royal started stirring in her sleep, I woke her up completely just to have time to eat.

Once we were all seated downstairs, we joked and ate. Ms. Owens was in love with "Silent Night" by the Temptations, so she had it on repeat back-to-back. Shit, we loved the song ourselves, so we didn't say anything about it. I even met Hasaun's baby mama, and she was nothing like I imagined. Shit, she could potentially be a new friend for me. She was humble and driven, and I loved that in a female. She was the perfect example of what baby mamas should be. She wasn't bitter, and neither was she salty seeing me hugged up on Hasaun. Shit, she bought her husband inside with her, and he even seemed like a pretty decent man.

∞ ∞ ∞

After breakfast was over and Hasaun had to go to work, I decided to hang out with my big brother Kyle since I barely spent time with him since I've been here. Kyle and I decided to have coffee at Starbucks while Royal stayed behind with Ms. Owens and played with Hareem.

Sitting across the table from Kyle, I could already see something was bothering him.

"What's wrong?" I asked, taking a sip from my caramel frappe.

"I'm stressed," he replied, running his hands down his face.

"You're stressed? Nigga you, the luckiest motherfucker on earth because you missed Thanksgiving. That shit would have really had you stressed, big bro." I laughed, shaking my head.

"I heard about you and Adrian. How are you really holding up? You tell me you're fine, but I don't know how true that is."

"I'm fine for real. I feel a lot better than before."

"That's good."

"Now, tell me about you. What's been going on? When am I gonna meet this secret wife of yours?"

"Hopefully on New Year's."

"Why New Year's?"

"She's white."

"What?"

"She's white, Tru. You know how mama feels about us dating white people. You know she's a lil racist. She ain't got a problem with white people, it's just us dating white people that took her over the edge, and you know that. You saw how racist her ass has been acting toward Todd when he first married Syaire. Would you wanna bring a white man home to meet Tiffany Garrett?"

"Sheesh, you right." I sighed.

"I know."

"But hey, if Syaire could do it, so can you."

"She's pregnant too."

"Oh Lord, but hey, at least y'all married."

"That's not all."

"Okay, what else is it."

"Aunt Jamie's husband."

"Oh Lord, please don't tell me you gay too."

"What? Gay, I ain't fucking gay," he replied, looking at me like I was crazy for just questioning his manhood.

"Well, Montray is. I didn't even stay long enough to know if he told mama and daddy or not."

"Yeah, he told me."

"So what about Aunt Jamie's husband?"

"So everybody thinks I work in construction. Well, I wasn't getting paid much, so for extra money, I dance."

"You dance? So you teaching dance class now or something."

"No, I'm an exotic dance, male stripper, whatever you wanna call it. Aunt Jamie's husband saw me on stage a while back. I think that nigga gay. I don't think he saw me see him but still."

"So you're married to a white woman and got her pregnant, and you're a male stripper. You selling drugs to toddlers too?" I asked sarcastically.

"Real funny."

"Look, if I could finally stand up to Syaire after all this time, you can tell mama and daddy about her."

"They probably still pissed that I missed Thanksgiving. I spent it with her. She's trippin' on me because we're not spending Christmas Together, and she's already nine months."

"You left your wife home while she's nine months pregnant."

"She's with her sister."

"Oh Lord, we gonna have a long talk."

Chapter 11:

WINTER WONDERLAND

Three Days Before Christmas

"You're still not gonna talk to me?" I asked Todd, watching him put Sunny's dress on.

Today we were supposed to be taking Christmas photos with my family and my mother wanted a picture with all her grandchildren in it. After Thanksgiving dinner, my mother wasn't talking to me or Nora. For some reason she wasn't as pissed off at Tru getting out of character. Thanksgiving was a complete shit show, and I prayed that Christmas was better. Nora went back to LA because everyone shamed her, and Adrian just walked around the house as if everyone weren't wanting to beat the breaks off his ass. I wasn't even gonna lie and say that Todd not talking to me wasn't eating me up inside. I even went cold turkey after that, and he didn't even care about that.

Shit, after all the time that I wasn't talking to Tru, it hurt me to know that Tru wasn't talking to me. Shit, I was even more hurt that she told me how she really felt. Tru and I weren't on a good foot the first time, but at least we didn't have that much bad blood between us than we do now. I even wanted to call her and talk to her, but I couldn't do that because my pride was in the way.

"There's nothing to talk about. I have to get Sunny ready. Are we done talking?"

"Todd!"

"What?"

"Why are you treating me like this? I said I'm sorry."

"Sorry doesn't solve what I could have helped you overcome just how you helped me. You hid everything from me! Everything!" he yelled, making Sunny cry.

"I'm sorry, baby. Daddy's sorry for yelling," he said, picking her up and soothing her.

"It wasn't something I could have just come out and told you. Todd it was hard for me."

"And telling you that I lost my wife and my child back then wasn't hard for me to tell you. So, it wasn't hard for me to tell you I was an alcoholic then. All you ever have is excuses, and I'm tired of it. Half of the time, you remind me of your Aunt Jamie. I feel like you're using me for money, like you don't even love me. Back at home you weren't trying to hear about what I was trying to say. You wanted to show the fuck off, like always. You barely spend time with me or the kids anymore, and I said nothing about it. You're quick to use my card and fly your friends out to do shit you can't afford to do.

Syaire, I'm retiring soon, and I'll be damned if I sit here and use my retirement money to fly you out to Paris to impress people who are only going to be there for you for that time being. You won't even fly your sister out and spend time with her. From what I've seen, Tru has been nothing but kind to you since you got here. You think I didn't see her ask you to come with her and shop for a present for your parents and you stuck your nose up at her like she was a disease. You're selfish, and I don't know how long I'll be able to put up with that. I had a heart attack worrying about you, and you couldn't care less. Bye, Syaire." he said, grabbing Sunny's diaper bag and walking out.

"Todd, I'm sorry!" I cried, trying to walk out but Montray stopped me.

"Give him some space."

"No, I can't. Why am I the fucking bad guy, Tray? Huh, why does everybody hate me? All I do is try to make everybody happy.

I try to make everybody proud, but they don't care. Is it me?" I asked, crying on his shoulder.

"I'm not even gonna lie and say it's not you because it is. He's right. Syaire, I love you, and you know that, but you most definitely can be selfish. You've been selfish your entire life. You see everything as a competition when it's not. I personally talk to mama and daddy myself, and everybody can admit that they treat Tru like she's a stepchild. Yeah, she's not perfect. She most definitely does put on this front that she's always happy when she isn't. However, if you know that she's not happy on the inside, and you know that you aren't, why worry about her? Ever since Tru has been back home, she has been trying nonstop to get into mama, you, and Nora's good graces. All three of you are selfish and need to get y'all shit together. Come on. Christmas is in three days. Get in the Christmas spirit and try and patch things up with everyone. I got you."

"Thanks."

"Don't thank me for something you should already know," he replied, kissing my forehead, walking out.

After taking family pictures, I received a phone call from Jessica, telling me that she was at a Motel 6 with Nora. I thought she was long gone after Thanksgiving, but the entire time she was staying at a cheap Motel 6. I knew my sister was down bad, but I didn't think she was down that bad.

When I pulled up to the hotel, all I could do was cringe my entire way up to the room. When I got up there, I knocked on the door. It wasn't even a whole five seconds before the door swung open, revealing Jessica.

"What's going on?"

"Nora's locked herself in the bathroom."

"What? Why?"

"Look, her boyfriend beat the shit out of her, and I followed her back here. She was crying in the bathroom, and she doesn't wanna talk to me. I need your help, and I'm worried."

"Fine, I got you." I sighed, sitting my Birkin bag on the bed. Walking over to the door, I knocked twice, letting what Montray said sink in.

"Hey, it's me," I said, putting my ear to the door.

"What do you want?" Nora asked, sounding as if she was crying.

"I'm your sister. I'm here to check on you."

"I don't need your fucking pity. If you're here to tell me I'm wrong, I don't fucking need you here."

"I'm here to check on you and apologize."

"Apologize?"

"Yes, I'm sorry."

"Sorry for what? You got so much shit to apologize for."

"Like what?"

"When I was younger, I always asked you to be there for me. You were never there for me. You were never there for any of us. You didn't sit back and babysit us. Tru did that. You were so stuck-up and fucking selfish, and all you worried about was yourself. You up and left to live with grandma while Tru raised us. You were the oldest, and you never acted like it. You never sang me to sleep, played with me, did my hair, or even fucking talk to me. You never acted like a sister, and you know it. You always tried to outdo everyone, and every time people try to get close to you, you fuck it up."

"I deserve that," I replied, sitting on the floor.

"Can you leave?"

"Not until you talk to me."

"I have nothing to say to you."

"Okay, we don't even have to talk about us, just tell me what happened."

"I fucked up."

"How?"

"It's Adrian."

"What? Girl, I haven't spoken to Tru since Thanksgiving. I'm pretty sure she'll be fine. I'm gonna speak to her about that later. Look, people cheat—"

"No, he did something stupid."

"What did he do?"

"Samson dead!" she cried.

"What?" Jessica yelled, running up and banging on the door.

"Nora, hun, what are you talking about?" I asked, hoping she didn't kill this man.

"When I left, Adrian followed me. Samson beat me because I didn't call him, and Adrian found out. Adrian was driving me back here, and he dropped me off in Dallas, so I had Jess come and pick me up. Samson found out where I was, and Adrian got to him before he could do anything. Adrian shot him."

"What? Where's Adrian now? Where's the body?" Jessica quizzed.

"I knew he left the house a few days ago and never came back. He never said where he was going," I revealed, getting up, pacing the floor, hoping and praying that my sister wasn't an accomplice to murder.

"I can't do this anymore. I hurt Tru, I hurt Adrian, all I do is fuck up!" Nora screamed, hitting on the wall, making me run over to the door again.

"Hey, stop it! Come on, please open the door. Let me in."

"No! Go away!" she screamed.

"No! Open the fucking door right now, Nora!" I yelled back.

"I just wanna sleep. I just don't wanna be here anymore."

"Don't talk like that, Nora. Come on, baby sister, open the door."

When things got quiet on the other end, Jessica and I began to yell and pound on the door like the police. Kicking off my Giorgio Armani heels and pinning my hair into a ponytail, I kicked the door open, not even caring about the agonizing pain that went through my leg. When the door opened, Nora was convulsing on the floor, foaming out of her mouth.

"Oh my god! Call 911!" I yelled at Jessica. I ran to Nora and pulled her in my lap, slapping her face.

"Come on! Get up! Get up for me!"

I dragged her to the bathtub and turned on the cold water, but before I could put Nora in, Jessica stopped me.

"Don't do that. It could put her into shock!"

"What? Then what do I do? I can't let her die! When the fuck is the ambulance gonna be here?"

"It's a traffic jam, so it's gonna take them twenty minutes to get here."

"Fuck this. Grab my keys!"

Doing as I said, I picked Nora up, thanking God she didn't weigh much. As soon as I opened the hotel door, it was snowing. It was fucking snowing. This was rare as fuck because is never snowed in South Carolina. We had ice storms, but snow was unusual, especially with it being so close to Christmas. I ignored the piercing cold concrete under my feet. Placing Nora in the backseat, I drove like a bat straight out of hell toward the hospital.

∞∞∞

When we arrived, they took Nora straight to the back. I didn't know whether to call my parents or what? I should have, but I knew how Nora was on keeping certain things to herself, and this was something I know for a fact that she would want to keep this to herself. My parents were already down her throat about being on drugs. Only Lord knew what they would do or say about her almost overdosing.

Christmas Eve

"Tru, you didn't have to come and pick me up. I would have found a ride."

"It's fine. Syaire was patching things up with Todd, so she took him and the kids out to eat. I wanted to come. I heard what happened."

"Hm, are you here to call me a crackhead and rub it in my face that I'm a skank?"

"Can you stop that?"

"Stop what? Tru, I did you dirty, and you're casually sitting here like ain't shit happened."

"I helped Adrian get out of a similar situation you were in, and I know how bad it can get, but I didn't know your situation was that bad. Look, I love Adrian, but I love you more. I already went years without being around the people I love, and I'll be damn if I sit here and do it again."

"I ruined your marriage."

"It took two. It wasn't just your fault."

"I'm sorry," I said, fanning my eyes.

"You're fine. Why didn't you tell me you were being abused?"

"It was complicated."

"Next time, speak up."

"Have you heard from Adrian?"

"No, but he's a smart guy."

∞ ∞ ∞

Instead of taking me straight home, Tru and I spent some time together. We got a booth at IHOP and decided to have some breakfast and hash things out.

"So, you're seriously not mad at me?" I asked Tru, cutting my pancakes in half.

"Oh, I'm most definitely a little pissed, but I'll be okay. I'm just happy you're straight. I know how it feels to be alone and depressed at times. I just wish I were the one there to help you. Are you gonna go to rehab?"

"Yeah, I am."

"Good, I'm proud of you."

"So, what now?"

"How you mean?" she asked.

"I know you with Hasaun? What's going on there? Or are you and Adrian gonna patch things up?"

"I think I'm gonna patch things up with Hasaun. Adrian and I talked before he skipped town, and we both agreed on a divorce."

"Wow, divorce." I sighed, still having the thought that I ruined my sister's marriage.

"Yeah."

"Why? You guys have a kid together."

"About that." Tru smiled awkwardly.

"Oh Lord, spill it, bitch," I said, taking a sip of my orange juice, then leaning in like a nosey ass big kid.

"Royal isn't Adrian's daughter. Hasaun is her father."

"Does Adrian know?"

"He does, and he wasn't happy at all. Apparently, he can't take what he dished out. That's why we both agreed on a divorce. Even if I agreed to get back with him, my trust would be too fucked up to be as comfortable as I was the first time. There's one more thing."

"What?"

"He said he loves you. I would never make him choose, and you know if I'm considered an option, I automatically don't want to be with a nigga. I'm nobody's option."

"Yeah. I'm just worried about him."

"I'm pretty sure he's fine. Stop worrying. Now let's talk about getting you into rehab," Tru replied, pulling a notebook from her purse.

"I got some help from Todd on some mechanisms he used. I know you're not an alcoholic, but hey, it's a start."

"Thank you."

"You don't have to thank me, it's Christmas Eve, it's snowing in the south, and you're alive. That's all that matters right now."

"I love you, Tru."

"I love you too." She smiled, reaching across the table to give me a hug.

$$\infty\infty\infty$$

After we finished eating, we went straight home. I decided on officially staying home and leaving the life I created back in LA. I was even debating on filling out college applications to pursue my dream of becoming a teacher. Since Tru was stopping by to see the family tomorrow, I had to face my parents on my own.

When I got there, I saw my mother in the living room watching *In the Heat of the Night*. Clearing my throat, she turned around and looked in shock that I was here.

"Nora? Baby, I thought you were in LA. I thought you left," she said, getting up and approaching me.

"I was. Can we talk? Where's daddy?" I asked, taking a seat next to her.

"Yes, of course, we need to talk."

"Mama, I'm sorry."

"It's fine. Look, I didn't get to talk to you how I wanted to talk to you because you just up and left me. It seems like all my kids like to run instead of facing their issues. When I ask you this, can you promise to tell me the truth?"

"Yes, ma'am, I promise."

"Was Syaire telling the truth? Baby, are you on drugs? Did you mess around with your sister's husband? Are you really broke?"

"It's true."

"Oh my god." She sighed, pinching the bridge of her nose.

"I'm sorry, mama."

"You shouldn't be apologizing to me. You should be apologizing to Tru."

"I already did."

"You did?"

"Yes."

"Baby girl, why didn't you tell me you were broke? Why didn't you confide in me?"

"Mama, have you met yourself? You're very judgmental. That's why we never told you anything while growing up because you judged us. You literally made me lose one of my closest friends. You knew that girl was gay, and you invited her to church and made her stand up in front of all these people while the pastor bashed her. Mama, you can be hypocritical sometimes."

"Well, I'm sorry you feel that way," she replied, trying to play the guilt card, but I didn't feel guilty at all for making her feel the way she was feeling.

By the time I finished telling my mother and father everything I went through, they were filled with rage, happiness, regret, and confusion. I was just finally happy that things were finally starting to change for the greater good.

∞∞∞

When nightfall hit, everyone was piled up in the living room, watching Christmas movies while drinking hot cocoa. It was as if Christmas was actually going to be looking bright this year. Todd and Syaire even made up. While everyone was watching *A Madea's Christmas*, I sat in the kitchen, looking out the window, watching the snow fall.

"Hey, what you doing in here?" Kyle asked.

"Just watching the snow."

"It's nice, isn't it?" he smiled, looking out the window with me.

"It's beautiful. I wish it would snow more often here." I smiled.

"Who you telling. I was just coming in to tell you to come in. Everyone is about to start opening one gift for tonight."

"Okay."

I followed him into the living room and spent time with my family for once, and it felt great.

Chapter 12

ON THE 12TH DAY OF CHRISTMAS MY LORD GAVE TO ME

Christmas

"Mommy! Mommy! Wake up!" Royal yelled, shaking me and pouncing on the bed. I groaned before letting out a loud yawn, turning to her. I smiled, seeing her curly pigtails bounce up and down. She looked so cute in her green onesie that was covered in little snowmen.

"I'm up, baby girl. Come on, stop jumping on the bed."

"We have to go open presents at grandma and grandpa's house, come on," she groaned, still trying to pull me off the bed.

"Okay, I'm coming, stop pulling me, go put on your boots and your jacket, it's still snowing outside, and it's cold. I don't need you getting sick."

"Okay," she replied, running off to rush and get dressed.

"Merry Christmas, Tru," Hasaun said, pulling me closer in his arms.

"Merry Christmas to you too." I smiled.

"What you got planned today?"

"Apparently, I'm about to head over to my parents' house to open some gifts with Royal," I replied, getting up.

All I had to do was slide on my UGGs since I had on the same onesie that Royal was wearing. Last night we dressed up in matching onesies and watched *The Polar Express*.

"Well, I gotta go pick up Hareem from Summerville."

"Okay, well, I'll be back here tomorrow. I promised my sister I would come over early to eat breakfast and open presents."

"Okay, I'll see you then, remember what I said."

"I will," I replied, throwing on my North Face hoodie. I gave Hasaun a kiss before grabbing my purse.

What Hasaun and I had was a work in progress. We knew for sure what we wanted. We just didn't wanna rush back into things. We were taking things slowly, and it was going just fine.

Instead of leaving right away, I let Royal open up a few presents Ms. Owens got for her. Even though it was last minute, she enjoyed every single one of them. While Royal was keeping Ms. Owen's company, I decided to make a long-overdue call. Stepping inside the bathroom, I dialed the number that was texted to me by Adrian's mother.

"Hello?" he answered.

"Hi, how you holding up?" I asked.

"Fine, thanks to you." Adrian sighed.

"Are you back safe in Mexico?"

"Yeah."

"Are you at the house I told you to go to?"

"Yeah."

"Good, I didn't want anything bad to happen to you. You know you can't come back here, right?"

"I know."

"I'm glad you know. Bye, Adrian."

"Wait."

"What?" I sighed.

"Thank you."

"You already said that."

"Look. baby, I still love you no matter what we go through."

"And you love Nora too, you made that very clear. I love you so much, Adrian, but I'm no longer in love with you. We already had a clear understanding of everything, so I think it's best if this is the last time that we talk to one another."

"What about Royal?"

"What about her?"

"Can I still see her?"

"Of course, growing up, she always thought you were her father, and I would never strip that away from you or her. Of course, traveling to Mexico back and forth is gonna put a dent in my pocket, and you know that. I'll try and have her visit you as much as possible."

"Thank you."

"It's nothing, bye, Adrian."

"Merry Christmas.

"Merry Christmas," I replied, hanging up.

∞∞∞

Royal and I made our way toward my parents' house, and all I could do was shake my head with a smile on my face at how she decorated the yard. There were blow-up decorations and lights galore. It looked beautiful, and you could even hear the music blasting from the inside of the house.

"Hang all the mistletoe
I'm gonna get to know you better this Christmas
And as we trim the tree
How much fun it's gonna be together this Christmas?
The fireside is blazing bright, wow
We're caroling through the night, wow
This Christmas will be a very special Christmas for me."

Chris Brown's version of "This Christmas" grew louder when I opened the door, seeing everyone dance in their pajamas.

"Royal!" Star yelled, running toward her and bringing her into a hug.

"Hey, Tru's here!" Syaire yelled, running up on me and bringing me into a hug.

"Hey, Merry Christmas." I smiled, hugging her back.

"Merry Christmas, TruBug." She smiled, calling me by my nickname. She hadn't called me that since I was a little girl.

"Y'all ate without me?"

"Girl, no, it's seven in the morning. Mama just finished cooking. The kids done woke the entire house up."

"I figured. Royal woke me up."

"Mhm, girl, these kids are something else. Come on, let's go open up some presents." She smiled, linking arms with me, walking with me into the living room.

Everyone was smiling, laughing, and still opening the hundreds of gifts that took up most of the living room. When I stepped foot in front of everyone, they jumped in excitement, pulling me in and shoving gifts in my arms.

"Girl, bout time, I thought your ass done dipped back to Florida after Thanksgiving," my Aunt Jamie said, passing me a present.

"I thought about it." I laughed.

"Hey sis, Merry Christmas," Nora said, rushing into my arms to hug me.

"Merry Christmas, Nora. Did you get my gift?"

"I did."

"And did you read the card attached to it?"

"Yes."

"Good, don't open it until tonight."

"You know I hate surprises."

"I know, despite that, this is a present you're gonna love."

"Hey Tru, can I walk to you for a second?" my mother asked, waving me into the kitchen.

"Of course."

Going into the kitchen, I saw that she already had the table set for everyone to just come in and eat. She had the house decorated so lovely that you would have thought she was in one of those Christmas commercials they play back-to-back on TV.

"How are you?" she asked.

"I'm fine, you?"

"I could be better, but I'm not. I have my family all together on Christmas, and I feel as if I still have tension brewing between you and Montray. I don't like having bad energy with my children. It took a long talk with the entire family to see that I've been unfair to you. I've been unfair to all of your siblings, and I'm sorry."

"Mama, it's fine."

"No, it's not fine. It was never fine. I tried to turn you into something you weren't — you, Kyle, Nora, Montray, and Syaire. We all know Marley's gonna do what he wanna do. I try every day with that child, but you know how that is. The thing is, I was always the hardest on you because I was scared that the world was gonna chew you up and spit you out. I wanted to raise you in the image I wanted you to be for me. I wanted you to be better than me. I know I lived a pretty good life, but I wanted you to live better. I have six kids, and my parents hated your father. I grew up being disobedient and not following what my parents wanted me to do, and it took all that mayhem at Thanksgiving for me to see that I was turning into my parents."

"That's all I wanted you to understand, ma. You pushed me to limits that I never thought I could go to, and in a bad way. You made me feel as if I was less of a woman for not following the foot-steps you put down for me. I felt judged for every little thing. I got married to a man I loved during the time, and I went to school and got my bachelor's degree when I wanted to stop at my associates because I knew I was stressed working two jobs, and I couldn't handle it. There have been plenty of nights where I passed out and starved myself trying to overwork and make you proud, but I just couldn't. Still, it took all that mayhem for me to also see that I don't have to live the perfect image because you want me to. I don't have to be competition with everyone because you wanted me to. All I had to be Tru, and from now on, that's what I'm gonna do, regardless of what anyone thinks."

"And I'll support you through it all."

"Really?"

"Yes really. Baby girl, I'm so sorry," she apologized, pulling me into a hug.

"That's what I wanna see. My two favorite girls hugging it out," my father said, coming in with his cup of black coffee. He joined in on the hug and kissed my forehead.

"I'm proud of you." He smiled, saying the words I always wanted to hear.

"Thank you."

"Come on, let's go be with everyone else."

"Wait, before we do, I need to talk to both of you. Montray has something to say to both of you, and so does Kyle. Do me a favor and give them a chance, please." I urged, looking at both of them.

They looked at one another with curiosity on their faces before both agreeing to give them a chance. My mother called everyone to the table, and we all sat hand in hand to say grace.

"Can I say the prayer?" Marley asked.

"No!" everyone yelled at the same time.

"Dang, I ain't even wanna say it anyway," he scoffed.

"Tru, baby girl, can you say grace?" my mother requested.

"Of course." I smiled.

"Lord, I would like to thank you for allowing my family to overcome all the obstacles we've had in our lives and to be able to gather and be around one another on your day. Lord, thank you for blessing the hands that prepared this meal that we are about to eat. Thank you for being the wall, the structure, and the bolder that kept our family strong through the issues we have recently overcome. Thank you for blessing me with supportive and forgiving siblings and loving parents. Thank you for blessing me with a family that conquers all. I pray for nothing but love, health, and growth for my family. In Jesus name, Amen." I smiled, opening my eyes, looking up at everyone smiling at me.

"To family," my father said, raising his glass of orange juice.

"To family," everyone said in unison, raising their glasses as well.

"Hey ma, dad, can I tell you guys something?" Montray asked, squeezing mine and Darius' hand under the table.

"Of course, baby, anything," my mother replied, sticking a fork full of eggs in her mouth.

"As you know, you all raised me to be the perfect man. I've done everything in my power to make you proud, and I feel as if when I tell you this, you're gonna be disappointed in me."

"Baby, we could never be disappointed in you," my mother replied.

"Oh Lord, Montray, you got a baby on the way?" my Aunt Jamie asked.

"No, I don't. I'm gay." He smiled, making everyone stop eating and look at him.

"Baby, your what?" my mother asked.

"I'm gay, mama, and Darius is my boyfriend."

"Oh, Lord, Jesus." My mother sighed, making me look at her sideways. She took a deep breath before reaching across the table and taking Montray's hand.

"Baby, as long as you're happy, I'm happy." She smiled.

"Really."

"Yes."

"What about you, dad?"

"Tru told me already. I was mad at first, but I came to accept it. I support you, son." He smiled, giving him a head nod.

"Oh my god. I love y'all so much," Montray expressed, fanning his eyes.

"Stop, don't cry."

"No, I just-, I'm just happy because I've been holding this in for so long, and I've always thought of the worse, and you all are giving me nothing but the best, and that's all I wanted," he cried.

"We love you, baby. We'll support you through anything." My mother smiled.

"I love you too, ma."

"We got you, baby brother," Kyle chimed in.

"So does anybody else have anything else they wanna get off their chest?" my mother asked, fanning her tears away.

Before anyone could reply, there was a knock at the door.

"Who could that be?" my father asked.

"I don't know. Maybe it's Ms. Owens, she told me she was gonna stop by. I'll go get it."

Getting up from my seat, I jogged to the door. Swinging it open, I raised my eyebrow at the woman that was at the door. Her straight blonde hair was pinned in a messy bun, and snow stuck to her black hat and scarf. You could tell she was freezing by the way she was shivering.

"Hi, how may I help you?" I asked.

"Hi, I know you might not know me, but I'm Emily. I'm Kyle's wife. Is he here?"

"Oh wow, come in, it's freezing," I replied, letting her in.

"Jesus, this house is beautiful."

"Thank you, did he know you were coming?"

"No, he didn't."

"Well, come on, I'll introduce you to everyone." I smiled, linking arms with her.

"Thank you."

I brought her into the kitchen, and everyone stopped eating once again to find out what this white woman was doing in our house. Kyle looked up and stood up quickly, rushing over to her.

"What are you doing here? Is the baby okay?" He asked the last question low enough for the three of us to only hear.

"The baby is fine," she whispered.

"Hi, uh, can someone tell me who this is?" my mother asked.

"Harpo, who dis woman?" asked Marley, imitating Squeak from *The Color Purple*. I could see the uneasiness settling in Kyle's face, so I decided to speak.

"Everybody, I'd like y'all to meet Emily, Kyle's wife and the mother of his child."

"Oh shit, Kyle said he got him a white woman. Todd's got somebody to relate to." Marley laughed.

"Shut up, Marley," Syaire urged, popping him in the back of his head.

"Hi everyone, it's a pleasure to finally meet you. I know this isn't the big grand meeting that you thought it would be, but it's most definitely a pleasure to meet you all."

"Nice to meet you too. I'm Syaire, Kyle's lil sister. Come sit down and eat. We have plenty of food," Syaire offered, getting up and helping her sit next to Kyle.

"Oh, wow, thank you."

All I could do was stare at my mother, who sat there, processing everything.

"So, Emily, where are you from?" my father asked.

"I'm originally from Short Hill, New Jersey, but I live in Madeira in Cincinnati."

"Oh wow, that's a very nice neighborhood."

"Oh, she a privileged cracker," Aunt Jamie mumbled low enough for only me to hear.

I kicked her under the table, giving her a look that could kill. It was no secret that she wasn't a fan of white women. A white woman stole her first husband, and she has hated them since then.

"So, you're pregnant?" my mother asked.

"Yes, ma'am."

"How far along are you?"

"Nine months."

"Oh Jesus, you're about to pop" You traveled from Cincinnati to here alone while you're on the brink of having your baby?" my mother asked, astonished at her actions.

By the way my mother said it, I knew she was calling Emily selfish in her head for not caring about the wellbeing of her child just to travel.

"I didn't wanna spend Christmas alone. Kyle was taking forever to introduce me to all of you, so I decided to take it into my own hands."

"I'm sorry, mama, I just wasn't ready for Emily to meet everyone yet," Kyle said, holding Emily's hand.

"I'm not upset. I just wish you would have brought her around earlier."

"I'm sorry."

"It's okay, so what are you having?" She asked.

"We're having a boy." Kyle smiled.

"Oh wow, congratulations, have you thought of names?" Asked Nora.

"Kyle Junior." Emily smiled, rubbing her belly.

"So, when's your due date?"

"Oh my god!" Emily gasped, holding onto her belly.

"What's wrong? Are you okay?" I asked, getting up from my seat to attend to her.

"I think my water just broke."

"Oh, hell no!" Marley said, causing my father to punch him in the shoulder for cursing.

And on this day, not only did my family sit together and repair what was broken, but we added two new members to our family: Emily Garrett and baby KJ, who was born on Christmas day. And most importantly, I got what I wanted, what I truly wanted — I got to be Tru.

Chapter 13:

DRIFTING ON LUCK

Syaire

New Year's Day

> *Your floor was damaged from months ago*
> *Where you dropped a hot comb dancing to neo-soul*
> *The trees are gold on your iPhone background*
> *Which is funny cos you cut down*
> *Like eight last spring for the new lawn*
> *How's it look, baby?*
> *How's it feel?*
> *Is it too much for you?*
> *~Choker*

It was New Year's Day, and Todd and I both decided to sit with a few friends of his and mine, along with a few recovering alcoholics and sexual assault victims. I didn't know how my husband put this meeting together on New Year's, but it was something I was happy he did. Todd and I recovered so much, and I couldn't thank him enough for not giving up on me. There was plenty of times where I treated him like less of a man, and I hated how I made him feel. I was no longer spending money like a bad habit, and I stayed home more to be with my family. I even cut off all the people who were using me. I felt like a completely new person, and I loved it. I didn't fully overcome what I went through because it wasn't something easy that I could do. It was gonna take a lot for me to get through, and I was happy I had an army behind me to support me through it. I even had a court date to fight my case against Uncle Larry.

"Hi everyone, I'm Syaire Nelson, and I'm an alcoholic and a victim of sexual assault. I turned to alcohol to numb scars that were still open. I'm a work in progress, and I've learned with the support from not only my husband but my entire family that I'm going to get through this." I smiled, looking over at Todd, holding his hand.

"Welcome, Syaire, we're here for you." My new mentor Layla smiled.

∞∞∞

After my meeting, Todd and I walked down King Street. Instead of staying in Tennessee, Todd and I decided to move to Charleston to be closer to my family.

"So, how do you feel?" Todd asked, pulling me closer.

"I feel amazing. I never knew it would have felt that good to talk it out."

"I know you would feel a lot better."

"Thank you."

"For what?"

"For putting all this together and for helping me."

"It wasn't just me. Tru was the one who made all the calls and set it up. We both came up with the idea, but she did most of the work."

"Wow, why didn't she tell me?"

"Because it wasn't for her to tell, come on, let's get back so we can set everything up for these kids."

"You got that right. We don't want Tyreke trying to set Star's ass on fire like he tried to do last year." I laughed, remembering how my son chased his sister around with a sparkler.

It was New Year's day, and I was waiting on my plane to land. Tru gave me a gift that snatched my edges like it was nothing. To think I would spend New Year's day in South Carolina with everyone else, but what I was doing now was better. I looked down at my belly, placing my hand on my child that was still growing.

∞∞∞

Once the plane landed in Mexico, I walked to the front of the airport to see Adrian holding a sign with my name on it. I ran into his arms, kissing him as he swung me around as if we were in one of those cheesy romantic movies.

"Oh my god, I'm so happy to see you!" I cried tears of joy.

"Me too. How did you get here? Can you tell me now?"

"Let's just say Tru pulled some strings. She got me a plane ticket to come here and gave me a couple of thousand."

"Tru did this?

"Yes." I smiled.

"Why?"

"Don't worry about why. She told me to tell you that she loves you, and you will always be her friend. She said to stay out of trouble."

"Wow!"

"Yeah, so where are you staying?"

"Come on, I'll show you," he replied, helping me into his 2013 Toyota Camry.

This was my first time in Mexico, and all I could do was stare at the beautiful scenery. The entire drive to the house, I bombarded Adrian with questions. We finally pulled up to this two-story house by the ocean. I looked over at him with my eyebrow raised. This man just killed someone, and here he was living lavishly.

"Wow, this place is beautiful, but how did you get it?"

"It was mine and Tru's first house. We built it from the ground up. Tru paid for me to remodel it, and I made it a home for us."

"Wow!" I replied, getting out of the car.

We held hands walking to the front door. He opened the door for me, and my jaw dropped in astonishment. He knew my favorite color was orange, and the entire living room was decorated in orange and white. The pictures we took together a while back were hung up on the wall, and he even had a few photos from when I was modeling hung up.

"This is beautiful."

"I know." He smiled, wrapping his arms around my waist.

"I always dreamed of this. I always dreamed that you and I would be together and starting a family. Who would have thought this would be happening?"

"We can work on starting a family tonight if you want." He smirked, kissing me.

"Well, you don't have to put in much work. You're already a daddy." I smiled, taking Adrian's hands and placing them on my belly.

"For real?"

"Yes."

"Quit playing with me."

"I'm not, I'm serious." I laughed, watching his face light up like a firework.

Adrian didn't even say anything. He picked me up and spun me around, kissing me. Who would have thought my luck would have drifted from bad to good just like that. I was definitely gonna give Tru a call and thank her for everything. That girl was indeed my guardian angel.

"Hasaun, can you give the girl some space, dang," Justina said.

"Nope, she finally agreed to be my woman. Do you think I'm finna let her go?" Hasaun answered, smothering me with kisses.

"Tru, just say the word, and we can jump him right now." Justina laughed.

"I'm used to it. He was always like this even when we were together then."

"Oh, Lord."

"I got some extra fireworks. Come on, y'all, before these kids beat me up," Justina's husband Nate said.

Hasaun and Nate carried the boxes of fireworks to my parents' house with my entire family sat in the backyard, adding the finishing touches to the food. The yard was so packed with family and friends that you would have thought we were having a family reunion. We had fireworks for months on end.

While Hasaun and the rest of the men were setting everything up, Justina, Syaire, Emily, and I were in the kitchen, helping my mother carry everything out to the back.

"Can I talk to you for a second?" Justina asked.

"Of course."

"I'm happy Hasaun and you got back together."

"Oh, wow, thanks."

"It's nothing. That man really does love you, and it shows. I'll kick his ass if he fucks up because you're a nice girl. You better be careful. He might try to put another baby in you, and he'll really trap you then." She laughed.

"Oh Lord, no, I don't need another child right now. I would like to wait awhile. I've got a lot of stuff to think about before having more kids."

"Take your time. There's no rush."

"Right, but kids are a blessing," Emily chimed in, rocking KJ, who cooed with his thumb in his mouth.

"Most definitely him, he came right on Christmas too. Keep him away from Marley. He's gonna have KJ collecting other girls' pacifiers like phone numbers in daycare," Syaire joked, taking KJ from Emily and kissing him.

"Thank you, Tru." Emily said.

"For what?"

"For talking to Kyle and practically delivering my baby. Well, you and Syaire delivered him." She laughed.

On Christmas, we were so snowed in we couldn't drive, and the ambulance was delayed due to that as well. Due to Syaire being professional at delivering babies, she got that baby out as fast as he made.

"It's nothing. Syaire did all the work."

"Girl, if it wasn't for you being so quick on your feet, I wouldn't have done it without you," said Syaire.

"Hey, y'all supposed to be helping me put this food out. Give me my grandbaby," my mother said, coming into the kitchen and taking KJ from Syaire. I already knew she was going to have him spoiled rotten. Emily might as well just give my mama that baby to have.

Once everything was set up, most people were eating while others were shooting fireworks. Hasaun and I sat by the pool while the kids ran around.

"So how does it feel?" he asked.

"How does what feel?"

"To get what you wanted for Christmas."

"It felt great." I smiled, intertwining my fingers with his.

"I knew it would."

"Hey everyone, I would like to make a toast before we start counting down to the new year," Syaire announced, coming to the middle with her sparkling apple cider.

"As you all know, getting our family together is like getting water and oil to mix. Thanks to my parents and my little sister, we were able to do something that we couldn't do for five years. I haven't physically been around all my family for five years, and I'm happy I got the chance to do that. Also, some of you may know that Tru and I weren't on a good foot in the beginning. However, thanks to her, I'm seeing things in a better light. Tru has been a big help for my entire family, and I feel as if she deserves recognition. Everyone, please raise your glasses. To Tru." she said, raising her glass.

"To Tru!" everyone cheered, raising their glasses and cups. Even the kids had their Kool-Aid Jammers raised.

"To being true to yourselves," I corrected, raising my glass of champagne.

We all counted down the new year, and fireworks were let loose like crazy. Even Nora was on FaceTime shooting fireworks and making a toast. Who would have thought all that mayhem through Thanksgiving would have brought us all together on not only a beautiful Christmas but an astonishing start to the new year?

"To new beginnings," Hasaun said.

"To new beginnings." I smiled, kissing him as fireworks lit up the sky.

The End

**WANT TO INTERACT WITH T'ANN MARIE & HER TEAM?
JOIN OUR READERS GROUP ON FACEBOOK @ *T'ANN MARIE
PRESENTS: THE HOUSE OF URBAN LITERACY*! WIN PRIZES,
BE APART OF LIVE BOOK DISCUSSIONS & MORE!**

Join Our Mailing List:

http://eepurl.com/gU81k5

T'Ann Marie Presents
is accepting submissions in the following genres….

URBAN FICTION

ROMANCE

URBAN ROMANCE

PARANORMAL

INTERRACIAL ROMANCE

WOMEN'S FICTION

For consideration, please email the first 3 chapters of your manuscript, synopsis & contact information to:

TANNMARIESUBS@GMAIL.COM

www.ingramcontent.com/pod-product-compliance
Lightning Source LLC
Chambersburg PA
CBHW071915120726
48001CB00005B/1749